SONDER

Jeslyn Benoi

Ansu Varghese

Caron Chacko

Editor: Jestin Joseph

SONDER

BY

Jeslyn Benoi
Ansu Varghese
Caron Chacko

Originally published in India

ISBN: 978-93-89540-36-9 (Paperback)
978-93-89540-37-6 (eBook)

Published by RIGI PUBLICATION

777, Street no.9, Krishna Nagar
Khanna-141401 (Punjab), India
Website: www.rigipublication.com
Email: info@rigipublication.com
Phone: +91-9357710014, +91-9465468291

INDEX

**Congratulations and best complements
from Al Ain Juniors School**

DANCING IN THE MIDST OF A LEGEND

"MELODY! What is the meaning of this" Luke threw the file comprising the statistics for the launching of Celestia's newest app on his desk, his face burning red with anger.

As General Manager of Celestia, Luke had to scrutinize the document and present it before the Managing Director. But Luke cast that burden on the Assistant General Manager and personal dog also known as me, Melody Walters, already drowned in paperwork.

"Have you finished the document certifying the legal alliance with Allet corporations?" he asked.

My face drained of colour at the mention of the form. I looked everywhere but at him. Who knew the wall had such minute crack lines on them?

"N-no. I haven't. I was about to, before you called me here." I defended.

Luke closed his eyes in frustration and slumped down on his chair. He rubbed his forehead and exhaled. He knew yelling wouldn't get the job done. So he sent me back to my office.

I grumbled about everybody being mean and that global warming was messing with their heads. On my way back, I hit the desk three times and almost cracked my little toe. My Inbox was flooded with e-mails and my computer hung up every three seconds. The pen scratched the paper as I was signing it and made a huge tear in it. I banged my head on the table after I had to write up the whole page again. Patience was an important requirement for my job, but as of now, it was running short. As was I, running I mean. I was pretty sure I'd have thrown my computer at the next person to enter my room. So naturally, I was disappointed. Surprisingly, I got the work done on time and requested to be dismissed from work earlier than usual.

Being an assistant general manager in one of the most famous multinational technology companies that specialized in internet-related services and products had its drawbacks. The managers were always in frenzy and under a lot of pressure to keep their company's standards high, which becomes directly proportional to the workload deposited on the rest of the employees.

My request for leaving early was answered in the affirmative. Who knows? May be Luke has a heart after all or he figured out my plan to smash someone's head with the nearest device. I didn't think he'd appreciate an employee casualty amidst all the headache he already has. I needed a vacation very badly.

I stepped out into the freezing air of Portland and smiled as I passed a group of Christmas carolers, singing with joy and enjoying themselves. I felt hitting myself wasn't a bad idea after I realized my car was still having its engine repaired in an automobile workshop, and I had already walked to the parking lot. Seriously, who in their right mind would design a parking lot 100 meters away from the building? Some engineer he was.

The cold wind swept my dishevelled chestnut-coloured hair back. My eyelids were forced close to protect my eyes from the dust. Fortunately, my formals entrapped the heat and kept my body warm. I waited in one of the waiting sheds for a cab to pass by, but for half an hour, none went by. I got easily annoyed when I was frustrated. My teeth clattered, signifying the increased drop in temperature.

In the distance, I saw a cab heading in my direction. But before I could hold out my hand for it to stop, it sped past me, my hair slapping against my face like a balloon man that went flailing around. Barely controlling myself from screaming in frustration, I straightened my hair. Between my failed attempts to keep myself from looking like someone who was run over by a truck, I noticed a cab that had parked right in front of me.

Thanking my luck, I stuffed my bags in and got in, calling out the address to my one-room apartment. I started tugging at my hair to untangle the mess. After making myself look somewhat presentable, I reverted my head to look at the driver, but to my surprise and horror, I found none. I rubbed my eyes thoroughly to eliminate any tricks my eyes were playing. However, I still found driver's seat empty. I flailed my arms around in panic and turned my head sideways to face the window and found that the car was heading in the wrong direction. This was not the route to my apartment.

A cab without a driver could be trustworthy right? Right. I was told that I am a serene and patient person. AT TIMES. I counted from one to ten to calm myself. Miraculously, it seemed to work, or it might be because I was too tired even to panic. I activated thinking mode and everything pinpointed in one direction. Not the boy-band. Something crazier than that.

When I was 6 years old, my mother used to narrate bedtime stories. Princesses locked in a tower, superheroes, Spider-man, genies and lamps, the girl that used a fork as a hairbrush and the list went on and on. One of the urban legends she used to narrate told of a cab that doesn't take you where you want to go, but where you need to go.

I rarely believed in myths, but in my case, believing was the only solution to keep myself sane, although, I still wasn't sure that my eyes weren't playing tricks on me. Sometime during my rant, I fell asleep. Way to go, smarty-pants. Fall asleep in a driverless cab.

I was forced to wake up from my dazed state when the cab jerked forward. I rubbed my eyes to regain focus and gazed around. I recognized the home from my childhood, the house where my parents lived. Instantly, I caught on with the intentions of the cab. It took me to my parents. The people I needed the most right now.

For the first few months after I moved to Portland, we kept contact. But as time passed, our interactions decreased. I became too busy with office work. However, I never forgot about them. They used to call me during the daytime, but I didn't have the liberty to pick it up due to restriction by the company.

As soon as I got out of the cab, it sped off, leaving me looking like a snow-woman in formals. The two-storied old wooden house looked the same with the well-maintained flower garden surrounding it. Fond nostalgia replaced the never-ending frown on my face with a smile.

I let out a sigh of relief as I took numbered steps towards my birth house. It was almost midnight when I finally had the courage to ring the old-fashioned bell. I heard footsteps rushing to open the door. Would they disown me? Hopefully they won't.

All my nervousness turned to joy when I saw the beautiful face of my mother rushing to hug me. My father followed to see me squished in the embrace of my mother, but instead of freeing me, he joined in.

After the long hug, my mother noticed my lush lips turning blue from long exposure to cold and from being rid of whatever oxygen I had left in my body, and placed me on the velvet sofa in front of the fireplace to get me warmed up. She got me a set of my old pajamas to change into and made me a cup of hot chocolate. I missed this. I missed being fussed over and spoiled, as childish as that was to admit.

I called Luke and requested a couple of days of leave. Surely, he could manage two days without his trusty assistant.

The request was rejected. He told me to return after the weekend. I should know better than to ask Luke for a holiday. I sighed. Well, then weekend it was.

I woke up from a nap and told my mother the missing detail of my story: the unbelievable part. After I told the story of my experience on the cab, my mother blinked and started laughing.

"Honey, your friend dropped you here, remember? She said she had some business in this area and you jumped on the opportunity to come here. You were dreaming." That explained it. I felt stupid for believing such a myth. A driverless cab that took you where you needed to go! Yah, and pigs could fly.

Later, I whined about the difficulties of my job and the effects global warming had on people's brains. They shared a confused look on the latter topic and my mother even had the audacity to place her hand on my forehead to check for fever. They eventually dragged me to bed after stuffing me with more food to last me a whole week. Ah! The comforts of being pampered. I was going to need new bigger sized formals.

I snuggled into my blanket as I thought of my silent and lifeless apartment back in Portland. My apartment was never a home, I realized. It was a house I temporarily took refuge in. Home is where people you love are.

Because in the end, it is the people you care about that makes everything worth it.

HOPE'S GIFT

'Waves lapping generously against the rough surfaces of the rocks, the wind challenging the ever-green branches of the trees to a duel, the small crabs and ants mimicking the action, birds flying in a formation across the vast blue mass they call an ocean; this really was the ideal last sight anyone could ever hope for.'

She stood on the rock with her dress playing in the wind, dreaming of all the things she would miss.

"Christine, lunch is ready." Marilyn announced. She turned around, smiled at her and joined her on the trek down to where the others sat.

When she had bitten down on the piece of meat, she wished she hadn't. It was always the same plain, flavourless and tasteless. It had been that way for 10 months. She hated it. She hated all of her hopeless life. It wasn't fair. She didn't deserve this. Ten months had passed since she discovered she couldn't be a normal eleventh grader anymore.

The news had shaken her to the core. All of her dreams had been crushed with that one word - Glioblastoma or brain cancer. She numbly accepted the fact; not having the strength to respond. Tears had abandoned her since then. All kinds of therapies abused her. Slowly, she forgot how pudding or chicken tasted and smelled.

An accidental eavesdrop had confirmed her life-span dropping to one or at maximum two years. She decided that there was no use of tying herself to hope anymore. She would only succeed in holding herself a prisoner to delusions.

Noticing her sudden withdrawal from life, her parents and friends suggested they went on a vacation. Wordlessly, she agreed. And here they were, on an inland island.

Christine scowled at the taste of the meat, or lack thereof. She could feel the meticulous stares and the drooping pity that hung in the air. Not feeling hungry anymore, she excused herself and went back to her previous support pillar. She stopped herself from reaching into her back pockets and fishing for a notebook and a pen that weren't there anymore. She loved to write; more so, when she was unsure of how she felt. It took her mind off things.

After she knew about her disease, she abandoned writing. What was the use anyway? She wanted to become a famous author and make people contented with her writing. But what use might it come to if she continued writing, her every second being numbered, not knowing if she'd ever been able to finish the story? Now and then, she wished she could continue her writing.

The rhythmic manoeuvre of the waves greatly calmed her. She wished she could drown in the depths of those bewitching waters as an escape from her cruel reality.

As Shakespeare once said, "Thou known'st 'tis common; all that lives must die, passing through nature to eternity."

So why not now? She could put herself out of misery, but something held her back; something that coerced her to reckon with herself.

Cutting out from her thoughts, she observed the change in the environment. A disturbance in the perfect symphony of the waves. An ant. She sat down on the wet sand to monitor its actions closely. Squinting her eyes, she noticed the small yellow mass on its back. Well, an ant has to survive, right? The ant was hurrying somewhere. Following its line of vision, a large rock faced her. But before it could reach the large dry mass, the residue of a wave engulfed it. She hoped it had a good life before it was taken away, unlike hers. Surprisingly, it wasn't sympathy but pure amusement that aroused in her.

The dead ant's movement caught her attention again. Except that, it wasn't dead. Astonished and more interested than ever, she watched the ant impatiently as it crawled across the sand trying to escape its impending doom. Unfortunately, the ant wasn't lucky enough. It got washed away by the current again. After getting thrown back for the umpteenth time, the ant picked up its speed. She smiled.

Christine sat it complete and utter dumbfoundedness. The world moved in its oh-so ever normal state, except for the fact that she has a hawser around her neck waiting to tighten its grip anytime, as she comprehended for the first time what had just happened. An insect hundred times smaller than her had just proved how wrong she was to lose hope.

Hope was a funny thing, you know. If it's broken, it leaves you in a state weaker than before. But if you permit tightening its grip, it could take you to amazing heights. A life without hope is hopeless. In the end, it all depends on your faith.

The insect's determination and faith had sparked a small fire in her; a fire to live; a fire to outsmart her disease. Do the ant know it had just saved a life from dying a worthless one? Not likely. But she was thankful. Such a small act but influencing a powerful meaning.

She decided she would continue writing. Whether she could finish it or not would be another question she would face when the time was right.

'While it may seem small, the ripple effect of small things is extraordinary' - Matt Bevin

IMPERFECT SYMPHONY

I WAS NOT HIDING.

I crept along the corridor, inching from one corner to the other. My emerald orbs sized up the shortening distance to my room. It occasionally darted from side to side, eyebrows scrunched up in concentration and anticipation. It looked like a scene from one of those movies where the main character was hiding from an oncoming disaster. But I was not hiding. I was merely being observant. Although, the disaster part was somewhat fitting.

The hallway was bare except for the furniture and a couple of hangers I took refuge in my haste. I tried to ease up my actions; I would not be accused as a creep. My heart was thundering in encouragement at my imminent relief when I crossed the final step to my door. It creaked slightly as I pushed the knob but before I could step in, a smug voice called from the opposite corner.

"Hey Rosie,"

I sighed. There goes my hard work. I was berating myself for even musing in my head about avoiding this encounter.

I dramatically turned around, clinging desperately onto the few seconds before I had to face him. My features crinkled when his irksome face came into view. Not that he was unpleasant to look at. He was a model, after all. Blue eyes, blond hair, a dashing smile, straight nose, and shaped eyebrows. The black leather jacket he wore complimented his white shirt and blue jeans. He was every girl's dream and my nightmare. The problem usually began when he opened that mouth of his. Hell would break loose.

"Aww! My Rosie doesn't have time for poor Ashy over here?" I looked up at his phony sad expression and pouty lips and closed my eyes. I counted from one to ten while mentally chanting, do not strangle him, do not hit him with the vase, do not kill him. It's not like I would have gone through with it either. I wasn't cold-hearted enough to end a pretty vase's life on a dumb-head. Besides, there was this small issue of losing my job and going to jail in vain, because nothing could crack his thick head. I took a long breath.

"For the last time, Asher, DO NOT CALL ME ROSIE AND LEAVE. ME. ALONE." Pausing at each word so it got through his thick skull that I was serious. Unfortunately, it didn't. Because he started speaking again.

"But where's the fun in that? Also, I know you secretly love the name." Did he have a death wish? Seriously, did it kill for him not to aggravate me in the mornings? Everyone knew I grew extremely cranky in the morning and that I ran my system on coffee. Speaking of coffee, there were new bend marks on the plastic cup in my hand that had suffered a better part of my wrath. And speaking of wrath, there was a certain person who would be a pile of ash if looks could burn. Oh, the irony.

"Please, just go find someone else to miff, Asher. I don't have time for your games." I folded my hands.

"You're right. You wouldn't recognize fun if it hit you in the back." Satisfied with his morning routine, he turned and stalked into his room shutting the door behind him.

I stomped into mine and plopped down on the revolving chair in front of the mirror. The expression of the girl looking back at me was unacceptable in her line of career. I smoothened the frown out the corner of my eyes and mouth. I looked like I could kill someone. I had a good idea whom.

I was not a morning person. Everyone who valued their head kept out of my way. Once I had enough coffee, my mood would change. A friendly, interactive and helpful person would replace the grumpy one. It was a good thing that all the shows took place at noon or in the evening. But he just had to kick it off with his opprobrious attitude and many others would endure the side-effects for it. I downed the last mouthful of coffee and slammed the empty cup on the vanity. I laid my head on the surface and closed my eyes, breathing deeply. Falling asleep on the job was one of my greatest flaws. Not always, but I could not help the exhaustion sometimes. This was one of those times.

I swatted at the finger jabbing between my shoulder blades and responded to a distant voice calling me.

"Rosie, get up. Shine's searching for you. You were supposed to be at stage five minutes ago for the rehearsal." I only managed to pay attention to the last part. My eyes blinked open and my head jerked up to collide with another. I heard him groaning. Serves him right!

"What was that for, woman? What did I do to you to deserve this?" I almost thought he was being civil.

"Being alive." I shot back, the scowl finding its right place again. He had the audacity to look hurt. His head had pulled back a few inches, and a hand clutched his chest. I rolled my eyes at his antics.

"I knew you were a meanie, Rosie, but I didn't know you hated me so much." He mocked. My scowl hardened. I shoved past him into the corridor and down the hall where I was about to receive a lecture about good sleeping habits and inhaling too much coffee.

"Try not to explode their eardrums with your ultrasonic scream out there, Rosie." His laugh echoed through the corridor.

"Try not to get killed. It'll be a shame if that happens without me there." I yelled into the hallway. He laughed again.

"Will do. You'll miss me too much if I die."

I was running now. I wasn't too sure that I'd be able to control myself if one more word had come out of his mouth. Fortunately, he took the hint and shut up.

The backstage was overcrowded, and I wiggled my way to Shine. She was our choreographer and my best friend. But that didn't mean she would excuse me if I was late. The brunette was shaking her head at one model and her brown eyes were edgy as she looked at me.

I broke into a huge smile, hoping she wouldn't be too angry. Surprisingly, she smiled back. Huh! That was easy. I was still cautious though. She was worse than a wrecking ball if you got off on the wrong foot with her.

"Looks like Asher got to you just in time. I was about to send the military army to wake you up, Rosie. Although, you could probably sleep through a World War." She teased. I rolled my eyes and grunted.

"Ok. Ok. I won't call you Rosie. Calm down." I knew I was testing the waters, but curiosity got the better of me.

"Aren't you mad that I turned up late?" I bit my lip anxiously, waiting for her to burst out any second. It never came. She looked confused until realization dawned upon her. She turned her mic off and put the clipboard down.

"Is that what Ashy told you? That you were late?" She held her phone up so I could see the time. It was 12:00 pm. I wasn't late. I was five minutes early. He was messing with me again. And I fell for it. Again. I covered my face with my hands and screeched into it. Then I started counting. One, two, three, four, five, six ----

"Actually, I was going to wake you up much sooner. He was the one who requested to let you rest until his turn was over. Something about you being too tired and angry to do your job without tripping on air." She was amused.

"I think he forgot to mention the part where he was the reason for it." I droned.

"Oh please! You're just saying that because then you'll have to be grateful for what I did." A voice arose from the back.

Speak of the devil and he shall appear.

He looked at me with an unreadable expression before smiling, "You're welcome." Being the ever-stubborn girl I was, I huffed and turned to walk away only to find Shine pulling me back.

"Careful! What is it with you and tripping over roses?" I turned my head to look at the rogue vase of roses lying around. Had she been a second late? I didn't think I'd be able to recover from that kind of humiliation. Again. Shine's shoulders were shaking with mirth, but a glare from me sobered her. She clapped her hands in authority and called the crew over for the setup for the next model.

My face could compete with a tomato for who has a darker shade of red and still win. I was safe from a lifetime of embarrassment, but nobody said anything about my prompt mortification.

I knew they weren't laughing because I almost tripped. They were laughing because that incident triggered their memory of another tragic story. Tragic for me, that is.

Half a year ago, our whole crew of models had gotten invited to the set of a shower gel advertisement. I had been beyond ecstatic. That had been my first time on an advertising set since I was on my job. When the recess stretched, I had followed my nose to an enticing fragrance coming from the bathtub on the set. There had been actual roses! I had been so giddy in leaning over to get a better whiff I hadn't noticed the wooden step that was attached to the bathtub. The next thing I knew had been splashing water everywhere when I fell face-first into it.

Hearing the ruckus I had been making, everyone gathered around the tub. Asher had been the one who had started the contagious laughing session. Shine had held onto a guilty face as she had been trying her hardest not to laugh while she handed me a mirror. I screamed. My hair had been sticking up in weird angles all the while housing several roses there. There had been one sticking out from underneath my ear too. I had blushed as red as the rose that day. That was how I landed with the nickname 'Rosie' - the one who emerged from amidst the roses. According to Asher, at least.

"Next up, Elain Scott," Shine called through the microphone professionally, all traces of laughter wiped out. Yes, my name was Elain Scott. Popularly known as Rosie. Said name gaining people a whack over their head.

I gracefully walked down the runway, looking out for anymore villain vases, and keeping an ear on Shine's instructions.

"One, Two, Three. Stop. Now pose. Retreat and repeat. Remember to smile. Yes, now do it again." Her voice echoed through the speakers.

After a few more perfected smiles, twists, turns, and poses, Shine dismissed me. I had to go back for another batch of rehearsal an hour later, so I took refuge on the nearby couch. I propped earphones in my ears and played a song. I was a music addict, and I had no shame in admitting.

Half-way through the second song, I felt one of my ear being more alert of the surroundings than the other. I opened my eyes to see Asher sitting beside me with his eyes closed and his head bobbing to the rhythm.

THAT'S IT. THAT WAS THE LAST STRAW.

I 'accidentally' kicked him while I tugged at the wire and trudged out of the room, feeling my anger thicken. I heard him call my name asking me to come back so he could know the name of the song I was listening to.

I went back to my changing room, as there was more time to kill. I could always go back when I was needed. I didn't know why I reacted the way I did. I was sure if it were anybody else, I would've shared my earphones. However, it was him, so I couldn't care less. I didn't feel any remorse. Except that I should've whacked him when I had the excuse to.

I didn't notice I had tangled the device up while I ran out. Finally, after what seemed like an eternity I untangled it. With a disappointed sigh, I noticed that one of the wires was dislodged. Bad luck seemed to have developed an unhealthy infatuation for me.

I made myself comfortable on the cushion and scrolled through my 'Funstagram' feed. I had a rather huge fan base. I weighed my decision of coming to rest on the sofa. It's not like I'd fall asleep, right? I did. I praised the good sense I had to set an alarm, just in case. I sat up groggily after the twenty-minute nap I had. The first thing I noted was that something was off. A white box which wasn't there before. I opened it to find a pair of brand new black earphones set inside. There was no note or any kind of message left behind to identify the person. Somehow, I didn't need one. There was only one person who had used my earphones before it was demolished. Asher. At least, he had the courtesy to replace it. Though, I had a part in it too. But whatever.

I walked to the backstage of Autumn Rains - that's what we were calling it - to see everyone in a frenzy. The tension and excitement were oozing out of everyone. It was supposed to be one of the greatest and largest fashion shows ever to be conducted. Everything needed to be perfect. A crowd accounting up to ten thousand were going to witness the show. And I was sleeping through practice. I really needed to cut down on my hibernation process 24/7.

My eyes screened the entire crowd from one length of the room to the other. I spotted Shine over by the stage instructing a model, but there was no sign of a certain blonde-haired person. Well, less trouble for me.

I made my way over to Shine to inquire about the progression of the practice. Anyone who had eyes and a brain could tell she needed a good break. She was over-exerting herself.

Sneaking up behind her, I started massaging her shoulders as soon as the model had left. She was the choreographer of the show but she was also my best friend.

"Where's the blonde bug?" I asked her after a few minutes. She tilted her head to give me a questioning look.

"He's getting some coffee......."

"Aww! Are you talking about me? Rosie, you are so considerate and caring. Bug? Please, you give me too much credit."

The two of them spoke at the same time and Shine stopped mid-sentence when she heard him speak.

I jumped back slightly at the unexpected voice from the back. I turned to glare at him. His hands were high in the air, protecting the caffeine from spilling on either of us when I turned. Before I could reprimand him about the consequences of sneaking up on me, he held a cup of coffee in front of my face.

"Coffee?" His face lighted up in amusement, sensing the mental battle I was fighting between accepting the coffee from my 'enemy' and rebuking him for startling me. The fight was in vain. Coffee always came first. Everything else could wait. Besides, he had already a fair share of tongue lashing from me that day.

I grudgingly took the coffee he offered me and took a sip of the delicious ambrosia while I watched him hand the other one over to Shine.

"Wait! What about you? Did you not say you were tired too, and that you needed a cup of coffee?" She looked at him questioningly. Even I pried my attention from my liquid lifeline after hearing Shine. Did she mean that he brought the coffee for himself but gave it to me considering my coffee addiction? I kept quiet, observing how this conversation was turning out.

"That's okay. I'll just go grab another one" He rubbed his neck and turned on his heel, barging out of the room.

Minutes later, Asher surged in with a new cup of coffee. He didn't approach me or didn't even seem to make eye contact with me. He just sipped his coffee and went on chitchatting with his friends.

I sat down and took out my brand new earphones. I admired it for a few long seconds before testing out its audio quality. As soon as the song started playing, I knew that those earphones weren't normal ones. These were high quality, putting my previous pair to shame.

I know I didn't believe it when I referred to him as my enemy. He didn't wish for my ruin or anything, just occasionally angered me, irritated, threw stuff at me, laughed, mocked - ok I needed to stop before I convinced myself to drown my former statement.

I drew near to him before I could change my mind and tapped on his shoulder.

"What do you want?" He threw at me rudely. I couldn't believe my ears. All this time, he sweet-talked and irritated me and when I finally decided to thank him, he acted rudely.

UNBELIEVABLE. Fine, if that's how he wanted to play it, then he doesn't deserve my gratitude.

My eyes widened, and I walked away with a snarl, getting a peek at his shocked face. He seemed to have realized his mistake a little too late. I had already reached the other side of the room. Right that second, Shine's voice boomed through the microphone.

"Mr. Evans, Ms. Scott, please conduct yourselves to the stage." Great!

Shine's foot was tapping in a steady rhythm by the time we got there. Observing my impassive look, she sighed.

"I am not working with him." I said.

"I didn't make the list nor can I do anything about it." Ok, so that method didn't work. So I went for the puppy's eyes.

"Elaine, you know I'm helpless," She slumped. I may not have wanted to work with Asher, but I would not let my friend suffer for it. I nodded.

Suspiciously, I felt Asher's presence behind me but he didn't say a word. He kept quiet. Can the world get any stranger? That was the time where he was supposed to say "Ickle Rosie can't handle my glorious self?" or "You're just scared you'll trip on roses again," with that obnoxious smirk of his. But, he kept a blank face and waited for my decision.

I moved onto the runway in silent acceptance and Asher trailed after me. Shine spoke out the instructions and we wordlessly fell into step. Something was wrong; he was too quiet that it was almost eerie. I knew I would beat myself over this thought later, but I preferred the noisy and annoying Asher to this quiet and awkward one. The silence seemed to stretch on for eternity until he spoke again. I almost sighed in relief. Almost.

"I'm sorry about before. I didn't mean to bite. I was just stressed out. What were you going to say before I knocked the words out of your mouth?" He chuckled grimly at the last part. I sneaked a peek at him. His eyes emitted sincerity and guilt. We were still on the runway, posing and turning, flicking smiles here and there, going full-on model mode.

"Oh, it was nothing. I just wanted to say thank you. For the earphones and coffee, I mean." I smiled. A real one, not one dipped in sarcasm and malice. I don't think I've shown this side of me often towards him. The shock reflecting off his face reassured the fact. He nodded.

Shine sent us off to get ourselves both mentally and physically ready for the show that took place just hours later.

I sat quietly as the makeup artist started working their magic on me.

Finally, the pre-show jitters that went missing earlier attacked. One thing I was proud of was my confidence. I could waltz in anywhere, anytime. So I didn't know why my role in the upcoming performance unnerved me. Probably, because that show could write my future. Many eminent designers were attending the show. My hands were slightly shaking, and I rubbed them to be discreet. I paced up and down and nervously glanced around. The noise from behind the curtain kept rising. She braved a peek at the crowd gathered there and swallowed.

My self-defence kicked up when I felt a hand on my shoulder and turned around imitating a fighting pose. It was only Shine.

"It's ok to be nervous, Rosie. We all have our moments. Why don't you have a glass of water?" I was too caught up in my trance I forgot to lecture her for calling me Rosie. I simply nodded.

I made my way over to the refreshments arranged for the participants and drank a glass of cold water, efficiently soothing my nerves. I started counting again, sensing no improvement even after the second set. By now, I didn't think my nervousness was completely about tripping in front of the audience or accidentally ripping the dress. I had a bad feeling about the show. Now, I was just over-thinking. What could go wrong?

The show started in 15 minutes and nerves had calmed down immensely. I was more confident. Suddenly, Asher showed up in front of me. Here we go again.

"Is that a bird nest on your head? And why do you like that joker from that horror movie?" He started laughing. I must have been possessed by a demon to have thought I preferred this Asher to the silent one.

"I'm not a mirror. Go do something productive instead of bragging about your looks. Some things can't be helped." I started to walk off. I didn't even have the energy to shoot a good comeback.

"Don't worry. You'll do fine." I heard him say. I turned on my heel to find him no longer there. Weird!

The show ran smoothly during the first round. Then, people started screaming from the farthest end of the crowd. Not knowing what was happening, I frantically looked around for some kind of explanation until a hand dragged me. Then we were running, from the backstage and out the door. The dress I wore made it harder, but I kept the pace. All around, I could hear gunshots and people screaming. The whole area was a disaster zone. My breath was coming in short but I couldn't risk waiting to catch our breath. My mind quickly wandered to Shine and all other models that could still be trapped inside the building. Briefly, I thought how about Asher was faring. Adrenaline rushed through me; I tugged my hand out of the grasp of the person holding it and ran back into the building. My friends could be in danger, it was the only thought that ran through my mind.

I didn't even have time to contemplate what was happening, when I was jerked back again and whirled around to blue eyes staring at me.

"I need to go back, please. T-they could be in danger. Let me go." I begged and struggled.

"Listen to me, Scott. They are all ok. You were the only left in there. What were you thinking?" He was angry. I didn't get to speak before he shook his head in a silent request to follow him.

Sprinting across the hall, we made it past the exit door again. The screams never lessened and the destruction never ceased. What was happening? Every gunshot triggered terror in my heart. That could be one of my friends at the end of the gun. I shook myself of the negative thoughts and jumped forward.

Suddenly, the window shattered from the inside and I braced my arms in front of my face to shield it. A few stray glass shards pierced my palm and knees, stirring a hiss from my throat. I fell, unaware of the looming threat. Everything happened in a heartbeat. A sound of a bullet piercing the air hit my ears. I strained myself to get up and ran as fast as I could to the origin of the sound. A tuft of blond hair, its owner hunched up on the ground was the last thing I saw before I fell to the ground, the increasing pain in my left shoulder numbing my head and my vision obscured.

I saw my parents, walking down the street with my hands in theirs. I saw the 8 year old girl licking ice cream at a parlour. I saw myself spending my time reading an old classic. I saw Shine and I laughing at a joke. I saw Asher, smiling at me. I saw myself laughing with everyone when I had fallen into the tub. I saw myself walking down a runway, showing off a dress. I saw myself bobbing my head to music with a smile on my face. Then everything went blank and my eyes rolled to the back of my head.

My eyes felt groggy and heavy, evading my attempts to open it. My body felt numb, as if it was detached from my head. I could not move. I was having a migraine, and I didn't have a way to soothe it. Everything was silent except for some machine beeping. My eyelids finally gave way and opened to a white ceiling on top of me.

I was in a hospital.

I heard the door open, and a nurse came into my line of sight. She scanned the monitor, gave me medicine and left after asking about my well-being to grab painkillers. The pounding headache released slightly, and I fell asleep again.

I woke up, feeling tired. Another improvement was that I could feel my body then. I wished I couldn't. I felt like a voodoo doll being pricked with needles and thread everywhere. However, the largest needle was thrust into my left shoulder. Lifting my hand to my face, I traced the white bandage wrapped around it.

"The glass shard pierced your skin deeply but you'll be fine." I jolted at the voice.

"What happened?"

"A civil attack. They hacked the security. "

"People didn't die, did they?" Asher kept silent. My vision became blurry again and a lone tear escaped before the painkillers took over completely.

They discharged me one week later, after they reassured me that my shot wound was healing properly.

A lot of shows were cancelled, but we still went back to work. Shine always looked out for me and didn't put too much pressure or strain on me. Asher never uttered a single word after the visit to the hospital. So, I decided to confront him.

After searching for him for half an hour, I gave up. He wasn't there. He turned up the next day and raised his eyebrows at me when he knew I was waiting for him.

"Where were you yesterday?"

"I wasn't feeling well." He replied nonchalantly. His eyes were bloodshot and not the same that twinkled with amusement and energy. He was swaying slightly, failing when he tried to cover up. His face was sagged. He genuinely looked tired. Suddenly, with a long sway he fell. I caught him before his head hit the ground. I cried for help and soon some of them came running and carried him to an emergency ambulance.

I sat at the edge of the room as he had before when the roles were reversed. I gave him some time to adjust to the surroundings when I saw him stirring from his sleep.

"Is there something you want to tell me?" I crossed my arms in front of my chest trying to seem intimidating but ended up looking like a puppy shaking with concern for its owner.

"There's nothing to it, Scott. I had been diagnosed with epilepsy all my life. I've lived with it. Case closed." He said with finality. It felt weird when he called me Scott. He spoke again after a few minutes.

"I have a lot of fans," Modest much. Ha. "But I don't actually have real friends, you know." He smiled.

"I'm sorry for all the times I teased you. I meant none of it. I just wanted a friend."

"Really! You had an amazing way of showing it. I would've never guessed." I bit back before I could stop myself.

"I didn't mean to ups—"He shook his head.

"No, no, it's fine. I deserve it. I wasn't the most amicable person to you. You know, you shouldn't have taken the shot meant for me. I might die anyway." He looked at me with an unreadable expression.

"Every time I tried to talk normally, all that came out of my mouth were insults. I don't know why. After a while, I gave up.

So, I kept my distance and kept silent. Now, I want to try again. Truce?" He held out his hand.

"Truce." I shook his hand and smiled. His hand was cold.

I stopped walking when I heard a melody being played on a piano. My curiosity got the best of me and I peeked into the room through the partly open door. A small child sat in front of the piano, her hands dancing on the tiles. The melody lost its sync in between and fell out of tune. It was imperfect. But it was perfect all the while. An imperfect symphony.

A few months ago, I might've called my life perfect. I had a perfect job, a perfect body and a perfect attitude. Now, my life was less than perfect. And I didn't mind that one bit. It was better that way. Besides, a perfect life would be utterly boring. I went back home happier than I ever was.

I spent my lunchtimes at Asher's hospital room. He was actually funny when the fun wasn't at my expense. I started seeing him in a new light. Soon, Asher and I became close friends. Shine, Asher and I went to the movies together, ate dinner at each other's place and often hung out. He still occasionally teased me, but I just laughed.

Months later, as I was walking out of my workplace to go see Asher who was on leave for a month, Shine rushed up to me and sobbed into my shoulder. Dread filled my stomach, Shine never got emotional unless something was grave.

I held her at arm's length and questioned her.

"Asher, he--" She sobbed.

"It was a seizure. His parents found him lifeless in the living when they returned." She cried harder.

I felt like I was being kicked in the stomach repeatedly until the air left my lungs. My hands were shaking and my lips were trembling. My eyes stung with tears and I kept myself upright with the wall as my support.

"What did you say? Surely, I misheard."

"I'm sorry, Rosie. I'm so sorry. It's true." I shook my head furiously. No, no, it was not. I was going to walk up to his place and see him lounging on the sofa complaining he was too tired to do anything else. Then, Shine and I would sit next to him and watch the new movie that she had brought. He'd comment about how nosy and annoying the main character was until I stuffed popcorn in his mouth to shut him up.

But, I just held Shine, both of us leaning into each other for comfort.

Even after three years since he died, not one day passed where we didn't think about him. He was right. I missed him a lot. His parting left a colossal chasm that could never be sealed. It also reminded me how much those small moments were worth. How much I would give to see him waiting in the hallway to make fun of me. Now, there was just silence, a heart breaking silence that went on and on.

But I learned to recover. The path was difficult, but I managed to thaw it. I was glad I decided to forgive him. Or I'd still be living in the dark with no clue of the person he really was. My memory of him would have been a fake, a façade. I would've never known the funny, friendly and helpful Asher. It taught me a lesson.

Even in the hollowest darkness, a little light could go a long way.

PIECES OF A BROKEN HEART

"Kid, what have you done? It's okay daddy's got you"

He stared keenly at the concerned father wiping at the ice cream stains on his child's dress as the mother stood holding the girl in her arms. The child giggled at her father's struggles. Unable to sustain his fatherly stern look, he laughed at the child's hysterics and took the child in his arms. She curled her arms around her father and hung to him tightly. The father adjusted his daughter on one of his arms and put the other around his wife.

A happy family.

Ethan turned away from cruelly jovial sight. A stuttering breath later, he found himself walking down the snow-covered pavement. He walked away from everything he wanted and could never have.

Sure, he could call his foster care a home and the people his family. But are they really? No. They had taken care of him until he had turned 18 but they'd never be able to give him the love he deserved.

He was found on the deserted corner of a street years ago when he was only half a year old. He got dispatched to the nearest orphanage so that he doesn't die serving as a satisfying appetizer for some wild animals or something equally horrendous. Overall, he was just an orphan. A nobody.

All these vandalizing thoughts haunted him as he ran down the bare street - his presence not on the street - but in the endless expanse of his thoughts. He often caught himself lost in these exasperating thoughts that he escaped reality through - a twisted and crooked reality. He didn't know why he kept reminding himself that he was an orphan. But he did. Even after years of realizing and accepting he had nobody, he still hoped beyond limits that things were different.

He wiped a lone tear that tickled down his face. He looked at the unfamiliar street he had run into in his state of despair. Huddling in a corner, he struggled to keep the cold from seeping in. His crimson sweater and worn out jeans did not help him keep the cold at bay either.

He did not look forward to going back to the hellhole of a house. After being gracefully kicked out of the foster care, one of his older friends who had already settled down offered him shelter until he could have his own. But every weekend and sometimes during the week his friends came over and caused nuisance through their frivolities. Today was one such day.

He worked as a waiter in a café nearby. Apparently, the manager had deemed him worthy enough with his 'acceptable charm' and mannerisms to handle his guests. He often observed different families that came in through the café's doors and often wondered if his 'family' would have been the same way. Some kids would grumble on about how their parents didn't buy them whatever they wanted. People often failed to realize the true value of something until it has been taken away. Only he knew how much he would sacrifice to have his family back. To have a family that would cherish him was his birthday wish every year.

"What are you doing sitting in the cold, lad?" An old voice woke him out of his reverie. He peered at the man's face. Where he expected to see the irritated face of a security, he saw the tender face of a concerned man most probably in his 50s.

"Just hanging around, sir." He casually replied.

"Sure boy! I'm thinking you don't mind having a few frostbites now and then eh?" he retorted. Ethan smiled.

"Come on up, lad." The kind man offered his hand. He accepted it and climbed to his feet. Ethan watched as the man removed a red scarf that hung around his neck and wrapped it around him.

"Thought you might need this. You were shivering." Somehow he had missed it. The man - whose name he later found out was Thomas - convinced him to make a quick stop at his house for a cup of hot chocolate. Tom - he said he liked being called - put a hand across his shoulders and steered him towards his home. Ethan could feel himself warming up to this man already. He felt a sense of security with him. But for all he knew, he could be walking into a death trap. Young adults were a pricey commodity nowadays.

Soon, they came upon a tiny wooden cottage amidst a snow-covered forest. No, not a forest; it just had picturesque features like one. A narrow path of cobblestones was cut in a perfect curve leading to the house. An array of flowers graced either sides of the road - primroses, tulips, jasmine, calendulas and other violet flower, yellowish on the inside with violet stripes emerging from the inside - coupled with herbs of all varieties. A wooden fence surrounded the house with a metal gate fixed at the end of the cobblestone path.

He had been so enthralled by the scenic view in front of him that he was unaware of Tom dragging him forward by the hand. He looked down at the cobblestones he was walking on. Each diamond cut stone disappeared with every step he took.

The door opened to a scrawny but tall woman at the other end. She could pass for a young woman if it weren't for the wrinkles around the corner of her eyes that betrayed her. Her deep copper hair fairly resembled his own.

She must've recently returned when evening hit home, espying that she still donned her work clothes. The woman glanced down at Tom's hand long enough to replace her calm module into a fiery look.

"You had one job, Tom, one job! Blimey, how many times do I have to remind you not to forget to bring back butter when you return from your aimless wandering? You sit at home all day long and venture out at midday to come back empty-handed. Then you complain all day long about me not baking your banana cake. It's always about you and your banana cake. Am I tired? Do I have to work from home? Have I eaten? No! It's your cake that's important... "

Was this what it looked like to have a wife? Ethan decided not to marry.

She didn't seem to have noticed him standing in the corner while she bubbled out her frustration at Tom.

"That's my wife," Tom leaned near to where I stood, still not taking his eyes off the angry wife.

"Figured," I replied plainly.

That was when she finally noticed my presence.

"Oh! Who is this young boy? I didn't know you brought company, Tom." She said.

"What's your name, my boy?" She smiled at him. Crazy ! how women changed faces in a nanosecond.

"Ethan, ma'am. It's pleasure to meet you." I replied tentatively, returning her previous gesture.

"Oh please! Come in! Come in!" She waved him inside the house. She still shot glares at Tom regularly. I couldn't help but smile a little at Tom's expense.

It was as homey as it got. In through the door, to the left, the living room lay welcoming as ever with its soft and comfortable velvet sofas lining the right and left corners with a huge couch of the same type in the middle lining the wall. A coffee table, crowned with a glass top was set in between the maroon sofas. A candle that was fixed on a table stand was lit.

On to the right side, a dining table lay barren with four chairs tucked into it. A clinking sound arose from the far corner where Mrs. Jatum was going about making something to drink.

The portraits and painting hung from the beige-colored walls. A good majority of them featured Mr. and Mrs. Jatum. He could be wrong, but judging from the intense details and exquisiteness, the paintings that inherited the space on the walls seemed to be works of renowned artists.

However, his eyes gravitated back to one photo-frame that hung in the midst of all the others. It introduced him to a young child, a baby who didn't appear more than a few months old. The child had a few tufts of red hair propping from its crown and green eyes. He radiated a bounty full of joy with his entrancing soft smile, with his small arms waving around and legs in the air.

Unexpectedly, there weren't any other pictures of the child on any of the walls. Not even one picture of his childhood or teenage years were present on any of the walls.

He decided not to question.

He settled to silently watching Melanie - he picked up the name from one pictures - walking around the kitchen, preparing the drink, while Tom had emerged from hanging his cloak on one stand. He wore a blue-checked shirt paired with black pants. His snow-cleared charcoal hair was neatly combed to the side. Black rimmed glasses rested on the brim of his nose, something that wasn't there before. It made him look older.

"Here ya go. One cup of tea for Tom and a nice cup of hot chocolate for you, dearie." she offered. He noticed she had shredded her earlier annoyance at Tom. Maybe, just maybe, he'd reassess his prior decision to not marry.

He brought the hot mug closer and took a sip. He would definitely reconsider if his future bride could make hot chocolate as heavenly as this. He had always been devoted to all things chocolaty. He instantly thanked the generous provider for the treat that worked its way to warm his stomach. The savory sweetness calmed him immensely, not that his undying love for chocolate has anything to do with it.

"Do you not like hot chocolate?" he asked Tom. Before he could get a word out, Melanie dutifully answered for him.

"He has a sugar problem. Diabetes of course. Besides, it wasn't unexpected. He consumed a bit too much sugar over the last years." Tom glared at her but kept mute. He nodded.

"What were you doing wallowing in the cold my dear?" Tom finally asked.

"I didn't want to go back," I answered

"Go back where?" His eyebrows scrunched up. Out of the corner of my eye, I noticed Melanie pulling up one chair nearest to Tom and seated herself on it.

I narrated my tale from the sofa I had taken my refuge. When I was done, I couldn't bring myself to look at either of them, so I directed my gaze elsewhere.

Next thing I knew, Melanie's arms were around me. I unconsciously hugged her back. Her warmth comforted me. My eyes drew back to the picture of the baby on the wall again. This time around, Tom noticed it.

"He was our sweet little bundle, our everything. Until he wasn't." Ethan didn't know if he wanted to inquire more.

So he didn't.

"Dear, why are you just skin and bones? We need to remedy that," He never considered that but okay.

They exchanged polite conversations and even had quite a good number of laughs at Melanie's tales on Tom's talent - that is being lazy - and Ethan finally left. On his way back, he wondered why Tom had invited him in the first place. Just because of the good in his heart, Ethan concluded.

None of Charlie's friends remained and there was no sign of Charlie either. He quickly locked the door and went to sleep, his thoughts running back in time to the comfortable little cottage and the company of the nice man and woman.

He found myself rapping at the door of the Jatum's the next day after his day shift at the café because of Melanie's exigency to rid him of his state of weight. 'To add some flesh in you', she had said. Tom had just smiled fondly at his wife then.

Melanie opened the door to a cup of hot chocolate waiting for him on the coffee table. Apparently, his craze for chocolate hadn't gone unnoticed by her.

He was still sipping the delicacy when Tom came down the stairs. The cold was still biting at his skin but the lit fireplace helped.

It was quite a while later that Melanie had ushered them to the dining table. Plates filled with mashed potatoes, fried chicken, salad, bread, orange juice and water was spread on the table. It was when he had placed a piece of fried chicken in his mouth that he realized the truth in Tom's word about Melanie's cooking. He gobbled down the meal and wanted a second helping but was ashamed to ask. Luckily, Melanie had done the job for him when she mounted another helping on his plate.

Later, she brought banana cake for him to feast on. Tom's eyes had gone as wide as saucers on seeing it. He had finally brought the butter. Or it could have been Melanie.

"Thank you, Melanie," she had asked him to call her that, "The food was absolutely delicious," he meant it.

"And thank you for inviting me," he added with a nod of his head.

He had removed his jacket from the stand when Tom spoke.

"It's late, lad. You can stay here for the night if you'd like," Melanie nodded in agreement. Honestly, he didn't feel like leaving either. So he stayed.

And that's how it started.

He became a regular guest at the Jatum's cottage during his free time. He spent time with Tom while Melanie was at work. Ethan finally got to join in on Tom's stravages and they went on expeditions to beautiful gardens, waterfalls, mountains, hills and forests.

He finally understood why they had chosen that particular location for their house and why their house overflowed with paintings of forests and oceans overlooking the sunset. He finally understood why Tom consistently forgot Melanie's grocery list. He was a nature lover. Ethan found himself enjoying it all more than he thought he would.

His ears still hurt from Tom's screams when the rollercoaster had whooshed at top speed across the water park they had once visited. Who knew Tom was afraid of a cart on wheels!

The next day he and Ethan had gone out and brought supplies for setting up a birthday celebration for Melanie. Her expression when she returned from work forever forged itself into his mind. Tom and he had gone as far as preparing dinner that day.

All things considered, they whipped up a delectable meal. Ethan had baked a cake, and they had sang 'happy birthday' before she cut it. Later that day, she hugged him with tearful eyes and confessed that it was the first time they had celebrated either of their birthdays in years. Tom added saying he wouldn't have been able to prepare everything if it weren't for Ethan's presence and help.

He also learned that they had just moved here a year ago. Canada was their home before they moved to Atlanta.

Before they knew it, Christmas had come upon them. Ethan tucked his presents between his arms on the way to the cottage he considered home. He wore a cream sweater over his red shirt. A green scarf that looked too small and worn out yet comfortable was wrapped around his neck.

He had owned the scarf from the time he could remember. It was still wrapped around him when he had been found on that street. It was all he had as a reminder of his childhood. The blanket he had been covered in had been long gone. He would wear the scarf every Christmas and on his birthdays. So he wouldn't feel alone.

He knocked at the door while balancing the presents in one hand. The lady of the house ushered him into the warm house which was enveloped in holiday cheers. He took a moment to appreciate the gleaming ornaments that hung from the Christmas tree. The house looked more festive than he'd ever seen it. It was a shame he couldn't help with the decoration. He quickly set down the gifts under the Christmas tree and plunged into the sofa. Had he not been engrossed in draining the warmth off the sofa, he would've noticed her smiling at him.

Tom plodded down the stairs heavily and sat beside him. He wore a jumper above a green shirt and a red scarf.

"Merry Christmas, Ethan," He said. Ethan returned the greeting. The rest of the evening sped fast, enriched with laughter, Christmas carols, nostalgic stories and hot chocolate. Dinner approached, and he removed his scarf and sweater and kept it to the side once he was warm enough.

A scrumptious dinner later, time found them seated around the Christmas tree to open their presents. Melanie and Ethan found Tom with a faraway look in his eyes. His eyes were on the sofa behind Ethan. Before Melanie or Ethan could turn to see what was occupying his attention, he leaned over and snatched something. He turned the scarf around in his hand and glazed his hand over the initials on the bottom.

"Where did you get this?" Tom asked, his eyes still not leaving the scarf.

"It's the only thing I have of my family. Why?" He explained. He looked over at Melanie to find her attention transfixed on the scarf too. He always thought those initials were of the makers but when Tom removed the scarf he wore around his neck and compared the initials to his, he knew he was wrong. It was the same scarf of different colours. Printed in grey, were the initials J.H.

Jatum House.

He looked at the kid on the wall who now looked more and more alike him. His heart throbbed with realization and looked at Tom and Melanie. With a wry smile, Ethan realized that the child in the picture shared his eye colour.

No! Father and mother, if his assumptions were right.

He glanced at the pair sitting in front of him for their confirmation. If he checked a mirror, he was sure he'd have the same expression as them. Their expressions radiated shock. The first one to react was Melanie.

She started tearing up and wrapped him in a fierce embrace. Slowly, his father did too. By this time, tears were streaming down his face.

They told him how their child was stolen from them at a young age but fate had other plans. He listened to their story, and it broke his heart imagining how hard it must've been for them, not knowing what happened to their only child. Not being there to witness him growing up and mature. Not knowing if he was alive and well.

There were his family whether biologically or not. And they fixed each other's broken hearts.

At least now, he could wish for something different for his next birthday.

THE LOST PEARL

"This is the final boarding call for all passengers booked on flight 156B to Kansas City. Please proceed to gate 6 immediately. The final checks are being completed and the gate will close in five minutes time. I repeat. This is the final boarding call for all passenger to board. Thank you."

The announcement rang through the speakers and it jolted me from my peaceful slumber in the waiting area. I could fall asleep anywhere and everywhere. It was a special skill.

I took a moment to appreciate the beauty of the airport. It was truly fascinating. It was not my first time in an airport. Trust me. Airports were my second home. My job required me to travel a lot, and I wasn't complaining. The intricate gold and silver designs on the walls were arresting. All the hard work and efforts put into it made it pleasing to the eye.

The airport bustled with energy. Parents having a hard time monitoring their over excited children and their surroundings, bachelors complaining about the inhuman prices at the duty-free shops, couples talking animatedly about their awaiting journey, young women still teary eyed from probable separation from their families or whatever other reason and others struggling with their trolleys. I smiled unintentionally and sighed. Such a remarkable sight.

Straightening the waist belt of my knee-length black dress, I clutched the handle of my suitcase and walked gracefully through the aisle. I tightened the grip on my valise as the airport staff handed my boarding pass back.

I triple checked my plans for once I am inside the plane as I walked along the jet bridge, connected my flight and the airport. Do some light reading, listen to music, eat, sleep for two hours, watch a movie afterward and kick-start a conversation with my fellow passenger here and there. It would be another normal day in the book of Camila Stevens and her travels.

Being the brand ambassador of one of the top fashion designer companies was not a piece of cake. It required a lot of attention and dedication. Not to mention a lot of travelling.

Tucking my suitcase into the overhead bin directly over my seat, I settled into the cosy and comfortable seat. I closed my eyes for a while. I could hear the flight attendants assisting the new travellers, people walking past her seat to find their respective seats and kids jumping with joy. I also heard someone dropping into his or her seat next to my window seat but I did not bother to look.

After a few minutes, everyone settled down and I could hear the distant voice of the airhostess apprising on buckling the seat belts and offering earplugs, scented wipes, candy and earphones.

It was when they reached my seat I opened my eyes, muttered a thank you after collecting my share of the items and turned to look at my partner. She had a mop of sleek, tousled blond hair unlike my own brown curls and had a hooded red jumper on that looked fashionable enough paired with jet-black jeans, the same colour as her eyes. She had earphones plugged into her ears as her head slightly bobbed to the music. It reminded me of an old friend.

'She seems nice,' I thought.

I worked on my exceptional talent, also known as sleeping, until I felt a jab on my forearms. I squinted my eyes at the troublemaker. It was 'her'.

"Hello! The name is Penelope Mase. What's yours?" She said with a sweet and encouraging smile.

'She was friendly and bubbly. Nice!' I decided again. However, she would definitely pay for waking me.

"Camila Stevens. Nice to meet you." I replied with an even sweeter smile. Being an ambassador had its benefits. You constantly needed to smile.

The girl's face scrunched up. Her eyebrows knit together and her lips puckered. It looked like she was thinking hard about something. I knew that look from somewhere.

The more time passed, the more awkward it got. I went back to my napping but something kept swirling in my head. I suddenly turned my head.

"Have we met before?" We both echoed each other's doubts. Both our eyes widened comically. I decided to test something out.

"A penny for your thoughts," I waited expectantly.

"Is that you, Mila?" She asked. Recognition spun in my eyes.

I smiled wistfully "In the flesh. Long time, no see friend."

I scanned her again, "I almost didn't recognize you. You look uglier than before.'' I kidded. She gave me a threatening look

"Why! I was trying to look like you.'' She smirked with a winning look reminiscing the old joke.

She beamed and then suddenly frowned. She might have been thinking of the way we parted.

High school had been at its peak. It was graduation time. The air was vibrant with all the students buzzing with excitement to send off another batch of students from their school. Everyone was running here and there with half held decorations, tinted papers lying on the floor, posters sticking out in odd angles, glitter and God-knows-what-else in girls' hair and some teachers taking responsibility while other bummed off at missing their classes.

I was one of those people who lie around doing nothing but acted as if I'm in control when somebody walks into the room. So was my friend. Penelope.

She was one of the best people you could have the luck of running into. She was the person who would laugh at me, and then hug me, after I scream seeing the words 'Based on a true incident' in a horror movie. Yes, I get easily terrified.

We were naturally funny. If you separated us, we would go abnormally quiet. You wouldn't even notice our existence. But if somebody made the huge mistake of seating us together, we would give the Krakatoa volcanic eruption a run for its money.

We were always there for each other through thick and thin. We created an unbreakable friendship. Or so we thought.

Eventually, our friendship started fading. For a reason I didn't know. We started breaking into fights over nothing. Slowly, we started paying each other less and less attention.

Sometimes when I passed along the bleachers, an image would appear. A memory; to stab me in the back.

I could imagine Penelope sitting there with a foul look on her face. I could imagine myself jumping on her and asking, "A penny for your thoughts?" She would push me away and say, "Its nothing, Mila." Ultimately, confiding in me later.

I had refused to cry. I had believed it was a lost cause. Drowning in emotion, I was ready to let our 12 years of friendship sink. I wouldn't be a burden to anyone. Besides, she was the one who started it, why should I bother to fix it. I made myself believe I couldn't care less.

Looking at her now, after 5 years, I felt pity. Not towards her, towards me. I pitied myself for not being strong enough to take hold of the reins of an uncontrolled withering friendship. For letting her slip through my hands like sand which once used to be strong like a diamond. A weak coward; I wished I could go back in time and fix what we had lost.

A valuable and precious friendship; a lost pearl.

I opened my mouth to say something but the woman with the food trolley interjected.

"Veg or non-veg?" The airhostess said with a welcoming smile.

"Non-veg." Both of us said together at the same time. We burst out laughing.

"Still stuck on those fried chicken balls, I see." Penny smiled nostalgically. We exchanged mindless banter until the airhostess had moved on. It felt like old times.

I realized I was too busy protecting my ego that I let a beautiful friendship tumble down in pieces.

We fell into a comfortable silence as we finished our meal. Penelope leaned her head back against the seat with her eyes closed. I tried to go back to sleep too. Tried. Somehow, I could guess Penny wasn't sleeping either.

I was proven right when she spoke to me suddenly.

"Why did we fight? What was the reason?" She asked in a pensive voice.

I remained quiet for a few minutes.

"I don't know." I answered honestly.

"Hmm," She sighed. She stayed silent for a moment and then burst out laughing. I turned my head in surprise, causing my eyes blink open. I sat there confused. Slowly, the laughter turned bitter, and then it turned into tearless sobs.

I put my hand on her hunched back in comfort. She craned her neck to look at me. All mirth was gone from her eyes. It turned sorrowful.

"Are you telling me we fought over nothing? That we broke apart for no reason," She asked.

"Yes." I said. She rested her head of the cushion on the seat. I did the same.

"I'm sorry," She said.

"I am too." I replied. And I was; for many things. I was sorry for letting her go. For looking past the long years of friendship just to save myself from shame. For not being a good friend.

We caught up on each other's lives as time passed. Apparently, she was an accountant in a bank. She was flying to attend the wedding ceremony of her relative in Kansas.

My five hours' flight flew past like five minutes. I did not listen to music, watch a movie or sleep. I was busy catching up with an old friend.

We exchanged our numbers and when the moment to bid goodbye dawned on us, Penny hugged me tightly. I returned it. We didn't need words to convey how we felt. I was glad to have her back in my life.

I would never make the same mistake again.

"I'm going to complain about the coffee served in the plane. It tasted awfully salty." Penelope complained as we walked towards the exit.

Some things didn't change though. I would tell her someday that I was the one who added salt in her coffee while she wasn't looking as payback.

BELITTLING LOVE

'Noisy' and 'boisterous' are the perfect words to describe a Friday night in Delhi. Cars honked annoyingly at pedestrians walking at snail's pace, wild music resounded from nearby pubs and, oh yes, there was the usual announcements of wares by street hawkers. And I, like any other young adult let myself be carried away by the sweaty throng of people around me. No, I wasn't here to partake in any of the cliché pleasures that folk my age ten to delve in. My mother was right beside me as we trudged along the grimy sidewalk, hurrying to the nearest supermarket. As the vehicles sped past me in supersonic speed, Mum instinctively grasped at my arm and pulled me along. I withdrew my hand. She looked at me, visibly in pain. But my eyes shouted loud and clear, I could take of myself.

Mum was not my type. It had been a regular occurrence in our household for her to get annoyed at the simplest of things that I did and she often reprimanded me for deeds she "assumed" I did. Back then, as a hormone-filled teenager, that hurt deeply. It was only at a certain point that I came up with a new tactic, 'Care less.' It was kind of like a retreat, keeping a distance from everyone and everything I loved, choosing to stay silent even if I was provoked to the farthest extent. I didn't want to use the word 'hate' to describe her. That, I felt, was too strong. Therefore, I went with: 'I dislike her.'

"Drink some water, dear. You look really dehydrated." I reluctantly took the glass of water that she offered me. My mother had changed over the years, but I hadn't forgotten the torture I had suffered during my teenage. She thought she could make me forgive her for all that she had done by sugar coating me with sweet nothings, she was unquestionably wrong. Two suicide attempts and a day away from them was what my parents' fabulous parenting had caused me to commit. Childhood was nothing but a terrifying nightmare. They had destroyed everything that I had loved in my life. Thinking that my friends were bad influence, they forbade me from talking to them. I was ecstatic at the idea of going away to study at a hostel. At least, all I had to face was the expectant faces of the teachers.

I am 21 now. Once a bubbly, happy-go-lucky being, I was now reduced to what they called a 'vegetable'. And I blamed my parents for it. To the world, everything seems normal – an admission at the finest institutions in India, a bright future ahead and a seemingly lovely family. But no one knew about the demons of haplessness that loomed our household.

"How was your little trip?" Dad smiled as he tried his hand at small talk. I nodded stiffly, implying that it was 'okay'. Something changed in his face to an expression of deep anguish that I was familiar with.

"Ankita, you know we're sorry about the past…When will you forgive us? How long will you continue hating us?" I knew they were sorry. But I was no longer the Ankita whom they knew to be ever-forgiving. Call me a sadist, but I wanted them to keep feeling sorry. Mum appeared near the kitchen door, sniffling. She had obviously been crying. I groped around my heart for signs of sympathy. Frankly speaking, I found none.

Taking my formula-fed, thick notebook with me, I ran to take resort in my room, hoping that they wouldn't pester me there. I slammed the door shut, a privilege that I never had when I was younger. Forgiveness was the last thing on my mind. I blinked back tears when I heard my mum whisper the same line that I had once whispered to myself, "Oh Dev, will this pain ever end?"

***

I paced across the sparkling white corridor, my heart racing and my lips chapped. Dad was sitting on a steel chair in a corner, his tears run out. After all, how long could a person cry? It was Dad who woke me up that morning, his face freshly-washed to banish any emotion from it. Mum had walked to the market for some groceries, without me this time, and a two-wheeler had recklessly forgotten to apply the brakes at the pedestrians' crossing. Mum did not have my hand to help her this time. A passer-by had informed the police as well as called an ambulance, after which my Dad was alerted.

Regret gnawed the back of my mind. Forgiveness was not something to be held back, I realized. It was something to be freely and duly given. When I had been referred to a psychiatrist after my two daredevil attempts at killing myself, the only thing that Dr. Thakur had told my parents was, "Never belittle love, even if sometimes, it doesn't really seem to be around." All along, I had forgotten that they were my parents. But some voice inside said, 'Once, they had forgotten you were their daughter too,' I pushed the thought away. Mum and Dad had tried to reach out to me so many times. But I had rejected their love, even though I knew they were truly sorry. Swallowing hard, I grasped on to the little faith I had in God and hoped everything would be alright.

The door of the ICU opened to pull me out of the death-like trance I was in. A smart-looking doctor came out. My Dad and I immediately walked up to him, hoping to hear good news, while also bracing ourselves for the worst.

"She has taken quite a fall, but there's nothing to worry about. A few months of rest and soon she'll be as fit as a fiddle." Both of us heaved a sigh of relief. I looked at Dad and smiled at him, probably for the first time in years. His eyes, glowing with happiness, were filled with tears. They were now falling not because of torment, but owing to the joy of the return of his prodigal daughter. Mum was going to be okay, Dad was happy, and if they were happy, I was happy too!!

***

We watched the waves as they frolicked and danced before us, with the salty air and cool breeze delightfully keeping us company. Not long ago, I had seen the sea and its waves as a symbol for eternal pain; the waves never stopped crashing on the beach and never broke its rhythm. But now, I saw it in a different light. The waves meant so much more to me – as a symbol of peace and tranquillity; every wave fell in harmony with my rejuvenated mind. Mum and Dad sat on either side of me, all of us eating roasted peanuts from paper cones. It was not just me who had been reborn over the last few months, but all of us. We had suffered much, but we were okay. I love Mum and Dad.

HOW THUNDER BECAME A LULLABY

I woke up in the middle of the night, frenzied with panic and quaking with fear. It was a thunderstorm. From my childhood, I have been apprehensive of anything related to the thin flash of electricity soaring through the sky, resplendent with stars. For some, it can be what might be described as a 'supercalifragilisticexpialidocious' moment, but I was perpetually living in the fear of Thunder and his associates.

Mum ran over and began soothing me with a string of words that seemed to connect together to form a gentle lullaby. I soon fell asleep, my ears still absorbing the affection evident in every crest and trough of the melody. The sky also seemed to drift into a silent slumber along with me, it's thundering and rumblings reduced to what sounded like the gurgling of a stream.

The previous night's fuss was soon forgotten like it was just a nightmare. My school was waiting for me as it always had, never changing, uncaring of whether children saw fantasies or horrors at nightfall. Class hours flew by. The whole day was spent on learning new scientific facts and of course, the latest gossip. Bus rides were the best. Some, overcome with tiredness, could be seen dozing off while the rest of us were engaged in excited, high-pitched rounds of chatter.

I was turned to stone. Nothing could explain the state my weak heart was in after I heard the news. It was as if my whole world had turned upside down. My mum was diagnosed with Stage IV cancer.

Dad, Lauren and Janice were equally terrified as I was. No one spoke. Somehow, the silence seemed more depressing than the news. Mum was her usual self, joking around, desperate to cheer us up.

"Oh, come on! I still have one more month to live!" All of us looked at her in bewilderment. How could she be so carefree when her 'Last Supper' was approaching? She rolled her eyes at us and sprinted into the kitchen. It was as though cancer had made her rediscover life.

As per her wish, a month full of 'lasts' was planned. A last wind-on-the-face feeling and the last goodbye were some 'lasts' on our list. Mum was extremely excited.

It was as though Mother Nature had taken time to make herself more beautiful. Waterfalls sparkled in the sunlight as if they had stolen the Queen's jewels. Fields stretched as far as the eye could see.

Mum is long gone. Yes, rough nights do come. The lullaby has been replaced by thunder, rocking me into a deep slumber. From that day onwards, the sound of thunder makes me smile. I'm no longer afraid of storms.

THE BROKEN BAT

It was a fine summer afternoon, one that was common to all of my city's inhabitants, who were now glued in their respective AC-fitted rooms, staring at the television screen just for the sake of staring at it. This highly disturbing phenomenon was not an unusual thing to come across these days - women talking nonsense just for the sake of talking, devotees offering various gifts before infamous deities without knowing the reason in doing so, children eating food while gaping at bright-lit 'iPad' screens, et cetera, et cetera. Unsurprisingly, this was what was happening in the Reddy household as well.

Cricket season was what most of us waited for the whole year. During those months, our top priority would be checking the scores on a minute-to-minute basis in some or the other app. Ladles and office documents would be kept aside for a while to give way to the 50-over match awaiting us. It was probably the only time when the whole family came together inside one room.

"India! India!" screamed the jersey-clad, more-than-thousand-pixels worth figure on the TV screen, namely Ranbir Kapoor. Cleverly made, the ad instilled an irrevocable sense of patriotism in us. Yes, today was the match we were all waiting for. India's first match in the World Cup. With advertisement-induced enthusiasm, we matched our breaths to the bowler's pace, crossing our fingers and praying for a "Howzzaatt!!" to ring through the sound system.

The first innings were over when 'it' happened. Probably spurred by the ongoing bat-ball tension and the above mentioned patriotism, my younger brother, Richard, asked me if I could play a match of cricket with him, outside.

Outside. What a beautiful word. Yet, many of us are almost always hesitant in it's use. We've always liked to abide with the opposite, inside. Curling up on a sofa and delving in delicacies at hand's reach are all that our shrunken brain can process these days. And when Richard said those ancient, unused words, I was caught off guard.

At first, I refused, like any other sofa-loving girl would. But he didn't back out. He pushed and pulled and did whatever he could to just get me out of the 'sloth bear' position that I had come to adopt. Some say rejection eventually wears you out. Whatever they said wasn't true for Richard at that point of time; he wanted to play cricket. With me. Outside.

I finally gave in, curled myself out of the cozy yoga-like arrangement that I had set my limbs into. One behind the other, we went into the garage and brought out the once used bat, ball and cricket stumps. Stored away for posterity probably, I thought and shared a silent laugh with myself.

After a languishing cleaning of the articles mentioned, we prepped ourselves for the match. He had Rohit's strategy and I, Kohli's style and consistency. It was a fair match by all means.

With the bat in my hands and sweat rolling down the nape of my neck, I looked like every other batsman to have ever walked down a pitch. With a smirk plastered onto my face, I poised myself to face the first ball.

A swing of his arm, and the ball came barrelling towards me. A sharp flick did it all. A loud thud was all I heard, and the ball disappeared into the bright yellow sky and I jerked my body forward to a run. Jogging my way through the temporary pitch that we had made, I laughed a deep, whole-hearted laugh - one that I had not used for time immemorial. I raised my bat in approval of the invisible spectators around me. It was a boundary.

Two matches and an injury later, Kohli won over Rohit with an unmatched margin. I was jubilant, the king's empire had fallen.

A second later, I decided I was tired. Taking the stumps and the ball with me, I walked towards my house, when the second 'it' happened. Richard wanted to play another match of cricket.

My breaths were uneven now. I didn't know what to chose, the previous decision hadn't been so hard. Keeping a straight face, mushy with sweat and dirt, I walked on, unheeding to Richard's broken pleas.

The bat lay on the road, waiting for its owner to return it to its rightful place. Richard's voice, now almost a sob, kept rising higher and higher, the treble in its tone threatening to crack any moment. Almost at the same time, a four-wheeler prowled around the street, prodding its wheels to turn toward our lane. Richard was now running, desperate to pull me back. I shrugged his hand off my arm and said, "No, I'm tired, I can't play." I could have. I should have. A mirror of his heart, the car sped over the sole bat that we owned, cracking it's very core to scattered splinters. Richard's piercing howl resonated in the air for what seemed like an eternity, as I stood on the verandah of the house, sorry for what I had done. Fixing two things at once was never my cup of tea - a broken heart and a broken bat.

'THE ROAD NOT TAKEN'

"Move aside, goofball!" I shoved Sam roughly to the side while we huddled into the car, as we set off to visit my new-born cousin. We've always been a close-knit family, though a stranger might perceive us to be distant and uncaring; it was just that we had weird ways of showing affection. Giggling, I sat cross-legged on the seat, shielding myself from Sam's playful punches. He was two years older than me, hence the MAJOR superiority complex. Ugh, brothers. But I loved him all the same. Dad turned the radio on to full volume, threatening to murder my poor ears.

The thing about Dad's driving is that you never felt a single bump, however uneven or pot-holed the road might be. It was also the perfect setting for a good, long power nap, but only if I didn't travel with Sam. Oh, travelling with Sam drove me crazy. We sang along with the radio, screaming out one of my personal favourites, Lord Huron's 'The Night We Met'.

Dad was talking enthusiastically to Mom when a bright red car came speeding our way. Sam noticed it first and launched himself at the steering wheel, swerving it to the left to avoid the imminent collision. My eyes widened as I frantically looked at Dad, who instinctively covered his face with his arms. All we heard was a deafening crash and then we slipped into oblivion.

Darkness. I was shackled with heavy iron chains and my eyes were blinded with some kind of a cloth. Struggling, I clenched my teeth as I heard Dad scream; the kind of scream that made me tremble from head to foot. I pulled against my bonds with all of my will and strength, until I fell forward in a heap, hitting my head on something sturdy. Darkness.

Everything hurt. My eyes felt groggy, as though they were tied to massive stones. I winced in pain as I tried to move my arm, sparking the attention of the nurse present in the room. Fluttering my eyes, I woke up to the sound of beeping machines all around me and people clad in white busily muttering incomprehensible things to each other. I was the only patient in the room. Where were Mom, Dad and Sam? I tried to recollect what had happened, but my head hurt too much. Tired, I dozed off.

"Careful, watch your step," the kind nurse held me as I took my first steps out of the hospital room. The treatment had made little difference; I was mentally scarred for a lifetime. A few days after my body returned to being normal, Mom and Sam broke it to me. Dad was gone forever. For hours, we held each other, mourning, and finding whatever solace we could in each others' arms. There had not been a single night when my pillow wasn't soaked with tears. Sam often held down my trembling body, as I bit into my pillow, trying to shush myself. Now, here I was, trying to relearn the same steps Dad had once taught me.

***

Three months later, we found ourselves in the police station. Before us stood the man who killed Dad, whether intentionally or otherwise. Hostility built up inside me, like a barred, angry lion pacing up and down in it's cage, threatening to break it open and slaughter the ones who held it captive. I could see Sam's eyes seething with fury. Mom sat on the wooden chair silently, her lips pressed together, lest they let out wails.

Silas. That's what his name was. Apparently, he had been rushing off to his 5-year old daughter's birthday party, while in the process he traumatised our family.

The court sentenced him to seven years of imprisonment. We had two weeks to deliberate on letting him go or letting him complete his prison sentence. Probably, the jury might have sensed how blinded we were by our grief and rage, that he put forwards this proposition. Sam was hell-bent on his decision. Silas had to suffer. Like we did.

Stepping out of the court, we headed towards our car to go home, but we were stopped by a pretty, young lady, approximately in her early thirties. She had a little girl in her arms, who was slowly sucking the lollipop held in her tiny fingers. The woman had eyes that looked like they were crying - red and puffed up. A strand of her long hair was stuck to her tear-stricken face.

"Please don't do this to us.." She folded her hands in front of us, her eyes threatening to overflow like a cup filled to the brim. It was only then that we realised that she was Silas's wife. Sam turned away from her and proceeded to enter the car, when the little girl caught onto to his shirt and said, "Do you know where my Daddy is?"

The atmosphere inside the car was contemplative. I could tell that Sam was in a world of his own, the child's innocent question still resounding in his ears. If we refused to let Silas go, the lady would have to fend for herself and her daughter. Alone. And that was not easy in today's world, where people could barely make their ends meet, even if their family was complete. I paused for a second, reflecting on my anguish after Dad's death. When he died, a part of us ceased to exist too. Yes, we had lost Dad, but did she deserve it too?

***

"Happy birthday to you!" We entered the brightly-lit house with gifts wrapped in brilliant rolls of wrapping paper. Aditi came running towards me, but then sharply deviated from her initial route to Sam, who was crouching with his arms wide open. I rolled my eyes and faked sadness by covering up my eyes, at which she came and wrenched my hands away and gave me the warmest of hugs. She was such a cutie.

Silas came up and hugged all three of us, impishly pulling Sam's cheeks. I smiled at them, because not long ago, things had been different. Lilly, Silas's wife, gleefully embraced us. We moved into the room, chatting and laughing, and for a moment, my eyes caught Sam's. We smiled, because we knew everything was alright.

EXPECT THE UNEXPECTED

The air was chilly and the wind was howling through the naked trees on a clear night sky, ruffling his dark brown hair. Josh tucked both his hands into his black coat pocket to keep them warm. The chilly wind was not helping his already shivering self but he ignored it.

Why ? You might ask..

It was because he was going to investigate a haunted house and needed all his concentration. He didn't have time to worry about chilly winds.

He has always managed to make himself scarce around a haunted house investigation but he was not so lucky this time. Was he even looking forward to this?

Let's just give that a big fat NO. Also, let's stop the rhetorical questions here.

But he had to do it. It was his job and he was not going to back out because of some haunted house nonsense. He unpinned his detective badge and kept it inside his coat pocket. He was in stealth mode today. Not Detective Josh. He was a common and ordinary man. He didn't exactly welcome the idea of broadcasting his identity during a case.

He sighed, his breath coming out as little white fogs. He was positive that a thing like haunted house didn't exist but there were no interesting cases coming up and he was just itching to have some action. As he came around the corner, he took his glasses off and cleaned it using the inside of his coat, all the while continuing his long strides.

Suddenly he bumped into something. He was about to fall but he regained his balance. Unfortunately, he lost his glasses during this episode and couldn't exactly see what was in front of him. He could make out the silhouette of a man but that was it. The man stretched his hand which was honestly blurry and held out something to him.

"Here's your glasses, Mr...er.."

"William. Josh William… thank you", he replied. He took the glasses and put it back on to see the man clearer. Or should he say a teenager. A very tall teenager, no wonder he looked like a man, given his sense of sight without glasses. He gave me a gun salute and went on walking.

'Huh. Strange. I thought no one lived around here.' he thought. He just shrugged it off and proceeded to walk on when he noticed a couple pass by him. He turned his head and looked bewildered at them who continued to walk forward. 'Guess I was wrong.' he thought noticing more people waking by. 'People do live here.'

He walked on shrugging his shoulders right in front of the main door. The house had been taped all around with warning signs which gave him some surprising calmness. Gathering all his concentration, he pushed the handle and entered the house.

The house looked pretty decent to him. There was dead silence all around, which was disturbed by his footsteps. There were a couple of creepy paintings around and a rug below the front door which said 'Enter at your own risk'.

Well, he already had entered the house without paying attention to that warning. It was too late to back out now.

After taking a step or two, he tripped. It hurt a bit and when he was about get up and take a look at the cause of his fall, he heard noises.

"Boooooo..BOOOoooooo.." He stiffened. His dark brown eyes darted to the sides and then the sound ended. Waking himself from the shock, he looked around for its source. He looked down and found the reason for his fall. A rope! He tumbled on a rope and fell. He experimentally pulled it and the spooky voices were back. Then he noticed that it was attached to speaker. He went over to it and pressed a button. The ghost voices were back.

Seriously?

But now, he was confused. Everybody who entered this house or looked at it from the outside had told that it was haunted. And he had come to prove that it was not. Didn't those people have brains to understand the simple mechanism behind the not-so-clever 'ghost sounds'?

He decided to move on and examine the paintings. He stopped in front of a painting with a mother and her baby, to examine it. When he looked at the mother's eyes, he saw them moving and focusing themselves on him.

Now that almost stopped his heart. What in the world?

He took of his glasses, rubbed his eyes,as well as the glasses for good measure, slid it back on, and looked at the painting. There were no more creepy moving eyes. The painting looked normal.

Huh. That's weird, he thought. I seriously need to get my eyes checked.

Then he spotted a room and decided to enter it. Upon opening the door, he saw a computer, complete with a keyboard and a mouse, showing different parts of the house,.

He went towards it and stood behind the rotating chair, peering into the computer. Then it dawned upon him that the entire house was being watched by someone.

Suddenly, he heard rustling behind him. He stiffened, but his mind was alert. His heart was thundering in his chest with anticipation, adrenaline rushing through his system.

He turned around to see a figure covered with white cloth which advanced towards him and howled, "Josh."

In his panic, he jumped on top of the 'ghost', tackling it to the ground. He removed the white cloth to reveal the person underneath. The person he saw brought his jaw crashing to the ground.

The so called 'ghost', whom everyone feared, was the same person he bumped into, while on his way here to the house. His face was now twinkling with amusement, with no hint, whatsoever, of the fear of being caught.

PICTURE PERFECT

It was a warm night with a slight breeze making it a perfect atmosphere to have a night walk. The air smelled fresh with the flowers that were blooming in the garden.

But she, who had luscious brown curls up to her mid- back, and bright grey eyes, with a petite body, was not seen.

She was stuck in the college library, trying to complete the assignment that was due the next day. She was not alone. Her best friend Sera and her brother Luke, who was a year older than both of them, were there, trying – emphasis on the word 'trying', to complete their homework as well.

The library was empty, except for them. The last person had just left with a suspicious amount of books. Might be a nerd. Anyways, everyone had gone to their rooms and was probably having a good night's sleep.

"Hey Jess, can you check the time for me, please?", asked Sera. Sera was literally one of the most beautiful and sweetest person and the sweetest person Jessica knew. That is, if you were on her good side. If you were on her bad side...Let's not get to that. It has only happened once or twice and, man, it was intense. She had black hair right up to her shoulders, with brown eyes and a not-so-pointed but fairly pointed chin.

"Sure." said Jessica, grabbing her phone from her bag. "It's 12:30. Are we doing an all-nighter?"

"Nah.", said Luke rubbing his eyes, seated opposite to Jessica. "I don't think I can keep my eyes open for another second."

"Alright.", said Jessica, grabbing her coffee mug and tossing it to Luke, who sleepily caught it. "We're staying for one more hour and then we're out."

Sera and Luke nodded.

Jessica tried to complete the rest of her assignment which was due.

Tried to.

"Hey guys", said Luke who had taken his phone out and was scrolling through it.

"Yeah?", we asked.

"I have a question," stated Luke looking at us with a mischievous glint in his eyes.

Uh! Oh!

Jessica looked at Sera beside her, who had a horrified expression on her face that mirrored hers. She assumed that the caffeine was messing with his system because she could clearly recall that he could barely keep his eyes open a few moments ago.

"Do you pour the milk first or the cereal?" he asked.

"Here we go again" muttered Sera.

"Milk, duh" sighed Jessica, answering anyway.

"What? Are you mad? It's the cereal!" said Sera with a bewildered look on her face.

"Right?" exclaimed Luke. "Who in their right minds would pour the milk first? This world has gone mad."

"Uhhh...hello? I'm right here. Wait. Why are we bothering to answer this question anyway?" Jessica asked. "It's like figuring out if it was the hen or the egg that was made first."

The two got right into an argument of which came first and Jessica sighed. Luke might be sixteen, but he acted like a five-year - old majority of the time. However, she loved him. He was the typical big brother. He had brown eyes and brown hair, with a dimple on his right cheek, which appeared only when he smiled.

"Guys, enough." said Jess, rubbing her forehead. "I'm getting a headache."

"Hey, did you guys hear about Brandon?" asked Luke. Clearly, he did not know how to follow simple rules.

"What about him?" asked Sera.

"He's the new captain of the football team." replied Luke. "I mean, why wouldn't he be? He's popular, smart, has good looks, is-rich and girls practically fall at his feet. I say he's the dumbest person alive in this entire college and he doesn't even have the proper skills to play football and –"

"Woah, woah. Slow down, bro. He's definitely not dumb. He has the skills to play football. You have seen him play yourself Luke. You're the quarterback after all. And admit it, he is a great football player.", said Jessica. After a moment, she said, "You're not... jealous, are you?"

"Whaaaaat? Psssh, no. Why would you even think that?", asked Luke.

She gave him a pointed look to let him know that she wasn't buying it and he sighed.

"Fine. Maybe I'm jealous. But only a little bit. I wanted to be captain too." pouted Luke.

"It's ok, Lu." said Sera, reassuring him. "You can get it next time. You do have one more year before you graduate."

Jessica nodded and he gave in.

"Let's just try to get this work done." said Jessica.

Suddenly, she heard a thud. Her eyes sprang open at the sound to see that Luke and Sera also were sitting straight and looking alert.

"What was that?" asked Sera. She was not a fan of horror stuff and being spooked was not something in her alley.

"I don't think it's anything. Probably some mice running around." said Luke, giving Jessica a pointed look, signalling to go with it. He was doing this for Sera's sake.

Jessica shook her head and went back to doing her assignment.

Thud.

Now, she went on full to the alert mode, looked at Luke and said, "That wasn't a mouse now, was it? Mice aren't this loud. That sounded like someone or something was dropped on the floor."

Luke could not argue with that. It was unmistakably creepy.

"Let's go check." Jessica said getting up and grabbing her phone.

"Uh.. How about this? Let's not go and check. You see, checking is going to cause a lot of trouble and uh... I mean what if we get caught? It's going to be a huge mess! What about our homework? We should definitely sit here and –"

Luke faked gasp and put a hand over his heart. "Are you...scared?"

"Uh.. Excuse me? Who are you calling scared? I'm not scared. Fine. Let's do this," said Sera, standing up with a determined face.

"That's the spirit," praised Luke, patting her on the back.

Jessica walked to the door with the flashlight from her phone switched on, while Sera and Luke grabbed their phones, switched on the flashlight, and joined her in the hallway.

She started trekking upstairs since they heard the noise from above them and the others followed. The top floor mostly consisted of labs and a few classes here and there.

They looked around the corridor and noticing nothing suspicious, decided to check each of the rooms. They started tip-toeing to the one on their right. It was the chemistry lab. They entered and looked around. Nothing seemed out of place. So they moved on to the next room.

They walked towards the next room which was the Computer Lab and –

"Oh my God!" exclaimed Sera, not so quietly. "Is that blood?" she asked looking at the trail of red drops on the floor.

"Hmm.", hummed Luke, kneeling to examine, flashing the light directly on it to view it clearly."Looks like it is," He sniffed. "Smells like it too."

He looked a few inches forward pointing the flashlight to that direction and found a trail of blood leading to the end of the corridor and turning to the left, right to the –

"Ok. So it's either the janitor's closet, or it's the spare room. Those are the only two rooms around that corner." pointed Sera.

"Ok. First, let us check in the computer lab. Maybe we'll find something," whispered Jessica.

Luke and Sera nodded, switched off the lights, not to let whatever was lurking around know that they were there, and they entered the room.

They could make out the whiteboard beside the door and with the teacher's desk right in front of it. The room had four tables lined vertically with computers set back to back on it, facing the students, kept on both lengths of each table. But the room was not as dark as a room was supposed to be when it was night. Some source of light was lighting the room up a little bit but not much. It was still dark.

"Hey! Look over there." whisper exclaimed Sera, pointing at the curtain-covered window. "It's slightly open!"

We looked at it, to see the wind blowing the curtain to the side and sure enough, the window was slightly open.

"Holy Guacamole!" whispered Luke excitedly, rushing towards it.

Jessica's stomach started rumbling. "Seriously bro? You had to mention food? Now my tummy's not going to cooperate."

"Shh. Stop being a baby and come check this out!" said Luke whispering.

"Ok, fine", huffed Jessica. And both she and Sera went to check out the window. When they looked down from it, they saw a rope, attached to a pipe coming out of the wall, just beside the window.

Sera looked at the ground, eyes widening, moving them across the floor, right to the door.

"Look! The blood starts from here, under the window, and trails all the way, under the door," said Sera, pointing at it for emphasis. "We must have missed it because the light from the moon did not illuminate the floor. Only the walls."

"She's right." said Jessica. "So something must have happened here and the injured person walked to the door and either went to the janitor's closet or the storeroom –"

"Or outside." interrupted Luke. "There's an exit over there. Remember?"

Jessica racked her brain picturing that particular hallway. Luke was right. There was an exit a few blocks away from the storeroom.

She nodded and at the same time, Sera said, "You're right."

"Alright people. Let's follow the blood trail." said Sera, marching forward.

Luke and Jessica shared an amused look before they followed her to the door.

She used a paper on the desk, to push down the door handle. She saw their quizzical faces because she said, "The handle is covered with blood."

Realization dawned on their faces and they nodded. Sera was one of the smartest girls Jessica had ever met. However, she only used half of it in her studies.

They entered the hallway, careful not to touch the blood and started following it to the –

Huh?

"It...stops?", asked Luke. "It doesn't go to the janitor's closet nor to the storeroom nor the exit but just...stops?"

Both Jessica and Sera had a similar bewildered looks on their faces. What's going on?

"Ok. You know what? Let's just check in the janitor's closet." said Sera.

We slowly tiptoed to the room, and Jessica held the doorknob. She whispered, "You guys ready? Cover me. In 3, 2, 1.."

She opened the door and turned on the lights to see –

"Woah! What happened here?" exclaimed Luke, with wonder.

There was a guy on the floor, lying against the wall, between brooms and buckets, with blood on his nose and all over his lips. He had a crumpled napkin in his hands with blood on both his hands and the napkin. His face looked blue and black, hinting that he had been beaten really bad and his wrist and his ankle were positioned in weird and awkward ways. Overall, the poor thing looked like a mess.

We moved closer to him and Jessica felt like she saw him fairly recently, but she couldn't recall when or where.

Wait.

He looked like the guy from the library.

"Isn't he Dallas?" asked Sera.

"Man, you can't even recognize the guy. He looks pretty out of it." said Luke.

"He's in my Maths class. He does look pretty beaten up." muttered Sera.

"But who did this to him? What is he doing in the janitor's closet in the first place?" asked Sera.

"I have no idea but first, let's take him to the infirmary. Lu, call the doctor. We'll ask the questions later." said Jessica and Sera nodded.

Luke put the call on speaker.

"Hello –"

"I'M TELLING YOU, LUKE PRESCOTT! IF THIS IS ONE OF YOUR STUPID PRANKS OR SOME SORT OF A PLAN TO DEPRIVE ME OF MY BEAUTIFUL SLEEP, YOU'RE DEALING WITH THE WRONG PERSON! I'LL MAKE SURE YOU'LL END UP IN THE INFIRMARY AND I WON'T EVEN TREAT YOU. GOT IT?!"

All of us closed our ears, to protect our eardrums from falling off. Great. He was in one of his moods tonight.

"I.. I'm sorry doctor. But this is no prank. This is an emergency. A kid named Dallas was found in the janitor's closet with blood all over him and his... his ankle was placed in a weird position and –"

"JUST SHUT UP AND BRING HIM TO THE INFIRMARY! IT'S TOO EARLY TO HEAR YOUR ANNOYING VOICE. AND LET ME GUESS. JESSICA AND SERA ARE WITH YOU TOO, ARENT THEY?"

"Hey, Doctor! Sup." said Jessica in an annoyingly cheeky voice.

"Hope you're doing great Doctor!" joined Sera, grinning.

"Ugh. God knows why I keep up with you lot." muttered Dr. James.

"Thanks a lot, Doctor! We –"

Luke was cut off by the beeping from his phone, signalling that the Doctor had hung up on him.

He sighed. "Great. Doctor's feeling cranky today. Whatever, let's just take Dallas to the infirmary, before Doctor gets there or I won't have my head where it is right now."

He pocketed his phone, picked Dallas up and carried him to the infirmary, followed by Sera and Jessica.

We switched on the lights and put him on one of the beds, waiting for the doctor to come. A few moments later, he entered the room with bags under his eyes, his black shirt, half in his blue jeans and half out, looking like a mess.

Guess that's what happens when you ruin his beautiful sleep.

He looked at them, annoyed, and checked up on Dallas. After checking, the doctor informed us that he had a twisted wrist and a twisted ankle, complete with bruised cheeks and chest and a bleeding nose.

"Also, I found this in his pocket." said the Doctor, holding up an inhaler.

Oh no.

"Was he asthmatic?" asked Luke, with a shocked expression, which mirrored Jessica's, and Sera's.

The doctor nodded, went back to his desk, and sat on his chair.

"Can any of you tell me what in the world happened?" asked Doctor.

Luke explained the entire story from the time they heard the noise, the blood trail, all the way to Dallas in the janitor's closet, with the girls adding the missing parts in between.

The Doctor was thinking hard by the end of the explanation. Then he said, "You guys head off to bed. I will inform about this to the Headmaster. If you need me, I'll be here for the remainder of the night. I want to be there when he wakes up."

All three nodded, went to the library to take their things and left the campus.

When the fork on the road came and they had to separate to go to the girl's and boy's dormitory, Jessica said, "We'll go to the infirmary first thing tomorrow. Lu, we'll meet you there."

Luke nodded; they shared their goodbyes and headed off to bed.

The next morning all three of them rushed to the infirmary to find the doctor, sitting behind his desk looking at some records. He looked up at the sound of their entry and said,

"I called the headmaster a few minutes ago. He is on his way." They nodded and he continued, pointing his head towards the bed. "He's awake."

All three rushed to the bedside, to see Dallas awake and sitting against the headboard.

"Hey. I'm Jessica, this is Sera and that is Luke. We were the ones –"

"Who found me in the closet all bloodied. Yeah. I know. The Doctor told me." said Dallas. He sounded ashamed and his voice was deep. He had brown hair, which looked like he had run his hands through, many times. He had grey eyes similar to Jessica's but dull, with thick lashes.

I nudged Sera and nodded. She nodded back, grabbed a stool, and sat on it, beside Dallas. Sera was an aspiring journalist. So I left the questioning part to the experts.

"Hey, Dallas? I know you're probably not in the mood, but could you tell us what happened?" asked Sera gently.

"Fine." said Dallas, when the headmaster entered.

"What's going on here?" asked Headmaster. He was a wise person, with a couple of white hairs on his head, which was a sign of his old age, and a big round tummy.

"Over here, Headmaster. We were just asking Dallas what had happened." called Luke.

Dallas exhaled, deeply. "Ok. So it all started yesterday, right after school, when Brandon came up to me and gave me his notebooks, asking me to do his homework. I said no, but he threatened to demote my parents from their position. We are not financially very stable. And if they got demoted, God knows what we would have done. And as you guys know, he is really rich and his parents have connections everywhere and are powerful. One phone call would be enough to leave my parents jobless. So I agreed. He also informed me that I had to submit the homework before midnight. He told me to meet him at the janitor's closet, and I agreed." he sighed and continued.

"I went to the library to complete it and was there till about 11:55, completing mine as well as his homework. It took a lot of time. In addition, I noticed that you three were there in the library, so I waited for you guys to leave before going to Brandon. But it didn't seem like you guys were leaving, and I didn't have much time, so I left anyway."

"I went to my dorm, left my books and my bag there, grabbed his books and left. I was walking around the building to figure out a way to get in because I couldn't get in back through the front door as the security had already seen me and had wished me goodnight. According to Brandon's orders, no one was supposed to even know about our encounter. That's when I noticed the rope. It was hanging from a pipe, near the computer lab window. Also, it was convenient because the lab was not too far away from the janitor's closet. So I put the books in my shirt, to leave my hands free."

He laughed humourlessly. "God knows what I was thinking. I'm not even a good climber and I'm an asthma patient, but I decided to do it anyway. So I climbed and reached the window. It was not locked so I quickly opened it and entered the room. But I stumbled on my way in and fell on my face. I got up, but I immediately felt dizzy and fell back down. I sat there for a few seconds, using my inhaler to calm my lungs and got back up. I left the lab, and went down the corridor, to the janitor's closet. But when I turned around the corner, I tasted blood. I stopped and felt my nose and lips to find that it was covered with blood. So I took a napkin from my pocket, wiped my hands, and covered my nose with it to stop the blood from flowing. It usually happened to me so I didn't mind."

"I entered the room and found Brandon standing there, scrolling through his phone. I took the book from under my shirt and gave it to him. That was an absolutely idiotic move. I should not have done it in front of him. He got pissed and started shouting at me for keeping his precious notebook under my shirt and that the book was of no use, because it was covered with my germs and that I had to write the entire notebook again."

"That was my breaking point. I shouted and told him that I wouldn't do it. He said I had just messed up and what he was going to do next, was completely my fault. Then he proceeded to punch the living lights out of me. And then I think I fell unconscious and woke up here in the infirmary."

He looked at the three of them and said, "I guess I owe you guys one. Thanks for finding me and bringing me here."

"You're welcome." they chorused, smiling at him.

"This is a serious issue. I'm going to call Mr. Crawford here." said the headmaster, before leaving us.

"Where's the Doctor?" asked Luke, turning around.

All three of them walked to his desk to find that he was sleeping, snoring lightly.

"Let's not disturb him. Let him have his beauty sleep." said Jessica grinning.

They went back to Dallas and made small talk with him. That's when the headmaster came in with Brandon, who was looking bored, his hands in his pocket.

Brandon Crawford was this typical good looking dude with blond hair and blue eyes, who was rich, popular and got girls practically drooling for him. I was not one of those girls and so wasn't Sera. That's why we were best friends.

The principal led him to the bedside and asked, "Anything you want to say, Mr. Crawford?"

His eyes momentarily widened before concealing it with a smug grin. Jessica just wanted to punch that smile off his face. Her blood was boiling.

"Oh hey there. How are your injuries? Hope you're feeling well." Brandon spoke.

"Mr. Crawford." the headmaster said, warningly.

"What do you want old man? You better keep your mouth shut if you don't want to lose your job." He said.

That's when Jessica exploded.

She went right up to his face and started shouting at him.

"Excuse me?! Who do you think you are, huh? What the heck is wrong with you? You think you can have everything just because you are rich? Huh?! We are in the 21st century! It is not like the olden times when the bridge between the rich and the poor was big. It's the freaking 21st century. Do you even listen to your history classes? Yeah right. You have your 'peasants' to do your homework, don't you? You are good for nothing, ungrateful, little brat. Do you think money can bring you everything? Even if you are a billionaire, and if you don't have love, you're nothing. Keep this in your mind."

"And if you think you can shut me up by threatening to kick me out of this school through your fame, you're wrong. I'm not like those other kids. If you want to kick me out, then fine, because guess what? I don't care. Just know that it will come back to you later. You know, you're such a coward. Hovering behind your parents and using them whenever something happens that doesn't go according to your plan. Pathetic." She spat.

She shook her head. "I thought you were different. I thought you were one of those guys who humbled themselves, and didn't use their money or fame to get things done." She chuckled humourlessly. "Guess I was wrong." And with that, she left.

Luke and Sera looked at Jessica's retreating figure, then looked at Brandon's shocked and gaping face. Then they looked at each other. Luke went ahead and slapped him on the right cheek. Sera went forward, and slapped him on the other cheek. Then they both turned and went in search of Jessica.

"What the –" said Brandon. He was too shocked even to form a sentence.

"Yes. Jessica is right. You should learn a thing or two about humbleness. You are suspended from school for a week. And don't you dare to threaten me. I was appointed as headmaster of this school by the Minister of Education himself. He's a just man and won't be bribed easily.", said the headmaster.

"I.. but I..", stammered Brandon, bewildered.

"No buts, Mr. Crawford. You're coming with me.", said Headmaster Thomas, dragging a still-shocked Brandon away.

Meanwhile, Sera and Luke were looking for Jessica.

"Where could she be?" asked Luke.

"Let's check our usual spot under the tree. She likes it more than me, because of the view and it gives her a sense of calm." said Sera. Luke nodded.

They reached the tree and sure enough, Jessica was sitting there with her knees drawn to her chest. They walked towards her and sat on either side of her.

Nobody spoke. Luke and Sera, gave her time to cool down.

"You know," Jessica started, "Even though he has money, there's one thing he doesn't have."

"What's that?" asked Sera softly.

"You guys. He doesn't have amazing people like you guys in his life. And no amount of money will ever be able to replace the both of you." said Jessica.

"Aww! Group hug!" squealed Sera. Jessica and Luke laughed at her silliness but hugged each other anyway.

"Time for a picture!" squealed Sera, yet again. Jessica and Luke, rolled their eyes at her, grinning all the while. Sera took her phone out and all three of them huddled together, while Sera held the camera away from them.

"3, 2, 1, Cheese!", all of them shouted together, laughing and grinning.

It was picture perfect.

THE UNEXPECTED HELP

Tall.

Humans are tall.

Why are they tall and not us? I don't like being down on the ground while they are up top.

And yeah. The temperature here is great. Cue the eye roll.

What am I you may ask?

Well I'm a dog. To be more specific, a stray dog.

Anyways, we dogs have our own little world. We strays live in hidden compartments under buildings or in secret passages and venture out in search of food. To be honest I'm pretty bored in here and am tired of searching for food every day.

Pet dogs have it easy. Their masters give them food and they are very comfortable in fancy homes. I'm not complaining about homes because I have my very own fancy room in my colony. I'm talking about the food. While we suffer for our food, they get it in silver platters.

Every day is a matter of life and death. Every step out into the world, is dangerous and fatal. There are dogcatchers everywhere, to catch a dog without a collar or identity and put them in pounds until someone decides to adopt them.

Our particular colony is packed with different breeds of dogs ranging from Terriers to Akitas. I'm Rufus, a German Shepherd. Like all dog breeds, we are uniquely vulnerable to certain diseases like Arthritis, Dermatitis, Gait Abnormality, Otitis Externa and skin allergy.

..What?

I'm not dumb. In fact I have a PhD in my very own name on it. Surprised? Heh...he. Humans are not the only ones with brains. We've got plenty.

Sometimes, I just go out and sit a couple of blocks away from a green bench, appreciating life in general. Pretty flowers, green trees, blue sky, laughing humans and cool breeze, all these elements make my day.

But that was ages ago.

Now..

From the corner of my eye, I noticed a mother hitting her child, anger evident on her face, and the poor child crying out loudly, hurt. The air was filled with smoke and dust. I couldn't breathe in a gust of air without some particles of dust entering my nose, which ended my nose in a sneezing fit.

In front of me, a guy was practically getting beaten up by a group of men who looked drunk. On my right, I..

Wait, What?!

I ran to the scene unfolding in front of me and started barking. The drunk men looked at me with disgust and the one nearest to me apparently had this brilliant idea to kick me.

Uh oh.

Shouldn't have done that buddy.

I growled at him and went right for his legs. The man whose leg was between my sharp and shiny teeth started screaming and pushed me off. And yes, I do brush my teeth before and after bed.

By this point, the others got scared and ran off with me threatening them with my barks. I looked back at the victim and saw that he had blood running from his lips and by the crooked way it was shaped right now, he had broken his nose as well.

Through all that, the guy smiled at me patting my head and looking bewildered.

"Thanks buddy." he said his hand continuing to pat me. "I owe you one."

"You're welcome." I said wagging my tail to show him that I liked it. More like barking because I'm pretty sure the only thing he heard is 'woof, woof!'

He seemed to notice my wagging tail because he started petting and rubbing my tummy, which I realized I needed and licked his face.

"Hey, hey, slow down buddy...that tickles." he laughed. I stopped licking and sat beside him while he composed himself from the ground and sat beside me. I liked this human. He had a jolly and good vibe to him.

"So what should I name you?" he asked and went thinking. "Hmm. How about Snowy?"

I gave him my best 'are you delusional' look, desperately hoping he understood. Like, excuse me?! I'm not even white. I'm brown. Ok? B-R-O-W-N. Brown! Get that into your thick skull. Not white!

"Ok, you clearly didn't like it..." he trailed off, noticing the expression on my face. Thank you Lord! I'm forever grateful. I promise to pray every night before going to bed, no matter how tired I am.

I looked around and right across the street, saw a big flex about some vet, but the thing that caught my eye is the name. It said Dr. Rufus right beside the picture of the doctor himself with a stethoscope around his neck. Perfect.

I got up excitedly and pulled his shirt signalling him to follow me. We crossed the street and I pointed right at the name.

Or... tried at least.

I was frantically trying to stand on my hind legs and point my snout and my fore limbs to the name. I'm pretty sure I looked like a mad dog.

"What is it buddy?" he asked when he noticed the name. "Oh! So your name is Rufus!"

Thank you again Lord! I promise to pray every morning as well.

I practically grinned and wagged my tail to show him that he was right.

"Wait, how did you... how come you.. !... you can read??!", he asked. His eyes about to pop right out of their sockets. He looked pretty funny to be honest.

'Duh', I thought, 'You'd be surprised at the things that I can do?'

I turned around and proceeded to go to my usual spot near the green chair. He still looked in shock before snapping out of it. He shrugged and came to sit beside me like before.

"That's a..uh.. pretty great name you have there..Rufus." he cleared his throat. "I'm Philip by the way. Nice to me – "

The ringing of his phone cut him off. He took it out of his pocket, looked at the screen and sighed.

"I have to go Rufus." he said patting my head once more.

I nodded. Hopefully it looked like I nodded. He gave me smile, promised me that he'll be back and left.

I left as well and returned to my house. Life was basically 'Hakuna-Matata' here. If you don't know what that means I don't know what kind of childhood you had without watching The Lion King. It's a classic!

I jumped on to my bed and lied down to sleep-

Oh no! I forgot to pray!

I quickly got up, recited my prayers, and went back to sleep where I was dragged into the world of dreams moments later.

A couple of days later, I was walking down the streets, hungry. I couldn't find food for the past two days and my stomach was grumbling loudly. I was almost fainting with hunger. It's times like this I think of getting caught and taken to the pound so that I could at least get some decent food. But then, the fact that I wouldn't be in my soft bed, which is required to get my beautiful sleep, takes me right out of that thinking track.

I would love to be a pet and all but what If I'm put in the pound and no one comes to get me? What if no human likes me? What if... what if I die there? Yeah. That's precisely why I don't plan on getting captured any time soon.

But one thing is for sure, I take food very seriously. If I have to go even a day without food, I get really cranky. Who's with me?

I mean, food is everything. She's my soul mate, the yin to my yang. I love her with all my heart. She's my sweet heart. I don't know how I would ever live without her.

That's when I smelled something. My mouth started watering at the delicious smell and my stomach grumbled yet again.

Don't worry tummy, you're going to be fed soon. Hold on tight!

I skipped my way, sniffing towards the smell. It was getting stronger and stronger and my stomach was dancing and shouting with joy.

There, right around the corner was a bowl filled with-

Oh. My. God.

Was that dog treats! I went closer and started sniffing; in the flavour of Chocolate Dipped Oreos?!

I couldn't believe my eyes. I thought I was hallucinating. Anyway, I was going to dive in when I stopped.

Wait. Who in their right minds would just randomly leave a bowl full of dog treats out in the open street? I looked around and put my brain cells to work. This, by the way, was a lot of work.

Why does this place look familiar?

Oh!

That was where I met Philip. See? This is what love does to you. It takes away all your ability to think rationally. There was a note under the bowl, which stated that the food was for me from Philip. He might have figured out that I could read. Clever boy!

That's when my stomach started shouting at me to eat it. What can I say? My tummy and I have a great chemistry. I proceeded to eat it and man! it was so damn delicious. That Philip kid just got ten gold stars from me.

Suddenly, I heard a group of guys behind me, laughing and shouting. I turned around and was met with the bunch of drunken guys from a few days ago.

'Great', I thought rolling my eyes. 'The drunkards are back.'

Immediately, one of the guys noticed me and his eyes narrowed in distaste. He pointed at me and shouted -more liked slurred in my opinion- at the others saying,

"Hey, isn't that the..*hiccup* same dog who.. *hiccup* biiiiit me on my *hiccup*...leegg?" he pointed at his leg to emphasize the fact and sure enough that section of his leg was bandaged tight.

Wow. I was actually impressed with this dude. He seemed to remember me even though I clearly recalled that he was drunk out of his mind.

"Wait." he said to himself, confusion evident on his face. "Wasn't that a dream?"

Never mind.

"Whatever." the man continued that little excuse for a dog is going to pay for what he did to me. Come on guys."

Uh, Oh.

They all started advancing towards me with menacing grins on their faces. I stood my ground and growled at them and for a moment they looked like they were going to poop their pants.

That's right people. I'm dangerous.

But it was only for a moment before they continued their advancement towards me.

What the..

Ok. I take that back.

That moment of shock was what they used to their advantage. The guy with the bandaged leg threw the almost empty glass bottle right at me.

Exhilarating pain shot through my head and I howled in unbearable agony. The other guys started hitting me with stones and more bottles. My vision was blurred and I could taste blood. I fell down on the ground and I howled and whined when a huge glass piece, which apparently was stuck on my back, got pushed further into my flesh on the impact. Tears formed in my eyes from the pain. I was weak and helpless. I could not do anything. Darkness started to creep from the corner of my eyes. The last thing I heard was someone calling my name before the darkness overtook my vision and I fell limp on the ground surrounded by a pool of red liquid.

I slowly opened my eyes to find a dog staring right back at me with a creepy smile on its face, which almost gave me a heart attack. What the heck – OW!!

I whimpered lightly at the pain I felt throughout my body and closed my eyes. I felt numb and I was pretty sure I was wheezing.

That's when I heard noises. I strained my ears and realised that two people were talking. I recognised one of them as –

Huh? What was he doing here?

I painfully turned my head to one side and opened my eyes once again. I noticed that I my area of vision had decreased and I could only see, though blurred, a particular part of the hospital, which was covered with dog wallpapers and toy dogs just chilling around the room. I turned my head a bit more, to my ultimate surprise, Philip was sitting with a man across the table. That guy with the white coat looked awfully familiar but I couldn't point out why.

That's when I notice the name card, where the words 'Dr. Rufus Bradley, Veterinary' was imprinted in bold, and gold letters.

Oh, now I remember.

He was the doctor from the flex, which I used to shield Philip my name, beside my green bench.

So a doctor named Rufus was treating a dog-named Rufus.

The irony.

I would have laughed if it wasn't for the situation I was in.

"There was a bunch of drunk guys attacking him and I couldn't just stand there doing nothing." explained Philip, while I listened with my eyes closed. "So I barged in and punched the living lights out of all five of them and gave an extra punch on their stomach for good measure. I mean, if they had drunk a little more of that alcohol, they would have passed out anyway. So, I didn't really do much. It hurt real hard but I was just so angry to care." he caressed his bandaged hands and continued. "I immediately called my brother who came with his car and we bought him here as fast as we could."

"That was very brave of you and thanks to you; we were able to save him." I assumed it was the doctor speaking. "If you had been even a minute late..." he trailed of shaking his head. "Let's just be thankful that it didn't come to that."

I shuddered and mentally made a note to thank Philip later. To be frank I've never met a human as nice and sweet as him. He was way too good for this world. I didn't know how to feel but now, I definitely owed him one. This could not be considered even with what I did to protect him. The only thing I did is bark and bite. I could have died if he had left me there. But he didn't.

I was brought back from my thoughts by the doctor's voice.

"He has a broken limp, minor cuts on his stomach and his head, two broken ribs, a major cut on his back and one of his artery was cut as well , but it's nothing we couldn't handle, and..he..umm.."

"And, what?", Philip asked with dread on his voice.

The doctor sighed. "And he is blind in his left eye."

I heard a sharp intake of breath but after that the ringing in my ears prevented me from hearing anything else.

I was blind.

No wonder my sight felt weird earlier when I tried to look at Philip, and I had to turn more than usual to see him properly.

I closed my left eye and opened my right. I could see, but not a wide area. Then I closed my right eye and –

Darkness. All I could see was pitch black. I couldn't believe it. I was indeed blind.

It was too much for me to take in and I let out a loud whimper. That's seemed to get Philip's attention because he ran towards me and hugged me tightly.

"I know buddy, I know. I've got you." he said. I opened my eyes turned and saw through my right eye that his eyes were glistening with tears. I whimpered again.

Philip started patting me on the head and said, "Don't worry, those drunken guys are in jail right now for animal abuse and for drinking in public." He continued, "Also, another thing. I'm adopting you."

I went still.

Philip was going to adopt me?

Me? Out of all the dogs out there... he chose me?

I'm guessing he saw my expression, because he smiled and said, "You're coming and living with me, buddy. I'll take care of you with everything I have. I promise."

This was officially the best day of my life. I wagged my tail as best as I could and licked his hands to show him my joy.

I love this human.

Maybe not as much as food – she is my sweetheart after all –, but close.

He laughed at my obvious joy and said, "Let's go home, Rufus.'